HUGH FOX

THE LAST SUMMER

Brian Buckley's Diary

For Dave,
Hugh
1995

XENOS BOOKS

Cover & design by Karl Kvitko

Library of Congress Cataloging-in-Publication Data

Fox, Hugh, 1932-
    The last summer : Brian Buckley's diary
        p.   cm.
    ISBN 1-879378-14-0 (hard). -- ISBN 1-879378-13-2 (paper).
    1. Cancer--Patients--United States--Diaries--Fiction. 2. Fathers
and sons--United States--Fiction.   I. Title.
PS3556.09L37 1995
813'.54--dc20   94-5380
                                                            CIP

Published by Xenos Books, P.O. Box 52152, Riverside, CA
92517-3152. Tel. (909) 370-2229. Printed in the United States of
America by Van Volumes Ltd., Palmer, MA 01069

INTRODUCTION

I've always liked the names of places like in England where they are authentic, not just superimposed on the landscape, but functional/historical. Like Oxford, derived from a real river which the oxen forded — Oxenford. Or in London's Southwork Cathedral, where the "south works" were, the southern fortifications of the English against the marauding Danes. Or like Sadler's Wells, built right on top of real wells.

These were the kinds of thoughts that passed through my mind as I drove away from Mount Hope Cemetery down Mount Hope Road after Brian Buckley's funeral.

Mount Hope was an authentic American place-name, the cemetery preceding the road and the Mount Hope Mall, and it was especially fitting for Brian to be buried there, I thought, because if you wanted to characterize his entire life, that would be the most fitting word to use — HOPE.

There were two focal points of this hope in Buckley's life, that of living to a ripe old age and seeing his children grown up, and that of seeing his unpublished work published at last. Neither of which, unfortunately, happened.

He had had six children, was happily in the middle of his third marriage when he died.

In fact, if you are to understand the diary he left behind, it might not be a bad idea for me to include some sort of family tree at the end of this introduction, where you can refer back to it as needed. The diary is FILLED with references to family.

Brian was 57 when he died (of lung cancer), and he left behind a tremendous amount of unpublished work — some twenty novels, books about pre-Columbian mythology /anthropology/archaeology, plays, stacks of poetry. Over the years he had arranged with Special Collections (first Jeannette Fiore, later Dr. Peter Berg) at Michigan State University to give them all his original manuscripts after he had made a typescript, although there weren't funds available to pay for xeroxing of the typescripts themselves, and he never got around to doing the xeroxing either — although he had always intended to. Of course, he had always expected to have years in which to get his literary affairs in order. He never expected to be cut off at the tragically young age of 57.

He had a kind of Job Complex, if I may coin a phrase. He saw himself as a modern Job who, after having gone through his sufferings and trails, would eventually end up on a sort of plateau of old age, surrounded by his children and children's children — and a tremendous amount of literary success.

Not that he didn't have considerable success during his lifetime. Over sixty volumes published, most of them poetry chapbooks. Enough, certainly, to stimulate quite a bit of subtle envy in his fellow writers here in the MSU literary community.

Ironically, all the local poets and writers had been at his funeral, although they'd maintained a certain jealous distance from him during his lifetime. In fact that was one of Brian's big complaints: "You can't get close to anyone, they've all got freon in their veins — they simply don't care."

They did care, perhaps a bit too much.

Unfortunately, they didn't show it while he was alive. Such is the nature of envy.

I even remember one time when he'd invited "The Gang" over when his son Chris was up from Kansas for Halloween ("I'd like to have the boy meet my friends, see me in my sauce!") and no one had come except a Cypriote, a Tunisian and two Japanese mathematicians, some students he'd invited as a kind of afterthought, "garnishing," as he put it.

There had been a Fall Birthday Club get-together among the rest of The Gang, and it had fallen on the night of Brian's party. F. Ronald Shanahan was supposed to have told Brian as a kind of spokesperson for the others, but it had slipped his mind. And no one called, no one showed up. He'd bought 25 pounds of Mexican sausage, and his students/former students had eaten some of it, and he fed the rest of it to his two dogs, slowly, over a period of months — like he'd wanted to keep remembering that night.

I'd never seen him so close to violence: "It's not just me that's involved, but the boy, my image in the boy's eyes, all the old-fashioned words — honor, shame, humiliation."

The boy meant everything to him. Christine's divorcing him had been the great tragedy in his life. In fact, when he was dying and they were trying to affix his lungs to the pleural cavities, some last-ditch sick doctor's futile experiment, I remember him telling me, "This isn't as hard as it looks. I've been dead since Christine left. All I'm doing now is finally lying down."

Which I more than understood. I'd been walked out on too — three years earlier.

Ten Little Indians — and then there were none.

The cancer had begun as a light cough that just hung on and deepened. Brian started taking antibiotics and began to lose weight, then his doctor decided to take X-rays, and there it was — the whole left lobe of the lung a massive, inoperable tumor. And it had already spread into the liver. They started chemotherapy, which wasn't only silly, but cruel. I couldn't believe how debilitated he looked when I went to the hospital to see him, like every breath was going to be his last, the effort he had to put into speaking. And to see him so emaciated. He'd always had a weight problem. "The Czechoslovakian Anti-Starvation Gene," he'd always called it, "for those long paleolithic winters." One month he was 57, looking like 40, the next he was 110.

When he finally was permanently hospitalized, when it was just a question of counting down to death, Christine, his second wife, came up and got Chris.

I ran into her in the hospital. It was still all "sides," for her or against her, no possibility of putting aside personal politics even when face to face with death.

She could have left the boy there until Brian had died, stayed herself, suspended everything else, just faced death and stayed. If Brian had a consistent philosophy of any kind, its core was the belief that early on in life, if you really come face to face with death, it will change the whole texture of your subsequent life.

Brian's first wife, Maria del Carmen Robledo, was Bolivian, and Brian had spent considerable time in the Andes and South American jungle (in Bolivia, Peru, Colombia and Venezuela) and had become quite an expert in South American Indian mythology, which in turn had led him to study prehistoric religion in the Old World as well. One of his unpublished manuscripts is called THE PALEOLITHIC MIND. *I've read it and was very impressed by it, a book mainly about the mythology of solstice-cycles in relation to ancient man's ideas about death and immortality. I've never understood why he couldn't find a publisher.*

When Chris was only four or five, before the divorce, but when it was already in the air, Brian used to take the boy to the same cemetery he himself was going to be buried in, and they'd look at graves, at dates, at how long people had lived, and Brian would reconstruct whole lives from just a few hints.

Like there'd be a G.A.R. marker on the grave, and he'd explain to the boy: "That's the Grand Army of the Republic, the army of the North during the Civil War. This man had been a colonel who died in 1864, just before the war ended, survived by a widow who lived for twenty more years, and a daughter who died ten years before the mother did. Probably not in childbirth or she wouldn't have the same name. *But I bet it was tuberculosis. It was very common in the nineteenth century..."*

I was with them that day when he did his little detective work on the Civil-War colonel. It impressed me a lot.

And I remember another time Brian telling me about another one of his visits to the cemetery.

"I'd said to the kid: 'You'll probably outlive me by fifty years. You'll have fifty more years after I'm dead.' And Chris had said: 'But we all come back, don't we?' And I'd stopped for a long moment, looking around at the falling leaves — it was late Fall and we were approaching the solstice — and all of a sudden it was 50,000 B.C., and my whole belief-system hinged on the idea of the yearly sun-cycle, and I answered: 'Of course, we'll come back. The days get shorter and shorter, don't they, but then there's a day when the sun stands still and they start getting longer again. Everything's in a cycle, isn't it?' That's what he wanted to hear. I don't know, even when he was three or four, he was always so twitchily bright."

I caught up with Christine in the hospital corridor.

"Listen, he's not going to be around for long."

"Keep out of it."

"I don't know, taking the kid right now. Maybe it's even good for the kid to be here when Brian dies — not to mention the effect the separation's going to have on Brian."

"So what do you hear from Holly?" she'd asked with a sneer.

Holly was my ex-wife. It was the overkill way Christine did everything.

"Nothing," I answered, "and I prefer it that way. I'm not much good with half-truces, half-wars."

No appealing to any common humanity between us. There wasn't any.

And then she was gone, the boy held tight by the hand, crying, trying to break away, "I don't wanna go, I don't wanna go!" But he didn't have a choice.

In Brazil in 1978, where Brian had been on a Fulbright at the University in Rio, Christine had brought Tanya home and told Brian she'd found a new friend (Christine had been Tanya's teacher in an English school in Copacabana) and wanted them all to live together. Brian had gone along with the idea and it had lasted eight years, and then the two women had fallen out, and Christine had left (always feeling that she had been forced out by Tanya) and found another woman (Mimi, originally Alsatian, a bio-chemist) who was at war with the world full-time. Brian and Tanya had stayed together after Christine had left, although earlier Christine had even suggested dropping Brian out of the threesome altogether and pairing up exclusively with Tanya. But Tanya wasn't interested at all in that. In fact I've always felt that Tanya got more into the "arrangement" because of her interest in Brian rather than anything she felt for Christine.

At any rate, after the split it degenerated into war. Christine became The Avenging Demon — get all the money you can, get the children, and (primarily) glut yourself on REVENGE, a revenge that didn't simply relate to the divorce but stretched back through Christine's life to a horrible, negative relationship with her own father that had colored her entire later life. Her father was an SOB, her father was a man — ERGO, all men are SOB's.

I'd never met the father (dead now about five years), but I'd gotten the picture: a sullen cowboy with lots of brains, who'd never had a chance to go to college and had ended up working his entire life for the railroad, frustrated out of his mind, taking it out, in his sullen, withdrawing way, on his wife and (especially) his kids.

Christine had become so embittered that she wouldn't have agreed to Chris's coming up at all that last summer if Brian and Tanya weren't essentially supporting her and Mimi, and if Brian hadn't threatened (more or less when the cough had first begun — almost as if, on some subconscious level, he knew that he had to make a stand now or never) to cut off the funds and fight her to death on financial grounds.

Although, to give credit where it's due, there was also the fact that Brian and Christine's daughter, Twyla, had cracked up the year before and ended up in a mental ward for six months, more or less directly because of having been taken away from her father with a court order. And Christine saw things globally enough to realize that the war between her and Brian was being fought on the battlefield of their children's sanity.

So there was a humanitarian element in Christine's letting Brian have Chris for that last summer, but, like he told me one night over some white Zinfandel over at Leonore Smith's place after a reading by Leonore at The Archives: "You can't help but wonder how Christine would have been if she and Mimi hadn't depended on me and Tanya financially."

*****

I was at Brian's bedside when he died. So was Tanya, and Brian's schizophrenic daughter, Barbara, was there almost to the end.

It had its inescapably comic overtones, Barbara being there, reciting menus like she always did.

"I had cheddar cheese and broccoli soup for lunch today down at Carter house, but it was so watered down that it was horrible. And someone had left the potato-chip bag open, so the chips had gotten all soggy, although the *fruit punch was good, and I always like cherry Jello with pineapple slices in it."*

Even Brian was amused, in the midst of all his agony, the last act in a life that he had always cynically referred to as "a total theater of the absurd."

He'd spent an hour a day with Barbara for years, and he'd always managed to limit it to never more than an hour — but now that he was captive on his deathbed, it was almost impossible to get rid of her.

She was on SSI, and had nothing else to do with herself but spend her days, years, whole life divided between stuffing herself with the worst kind of junk food and getting anti-psychotic drug shots, and TALKING about eating and taking shots. The State of Michigan had even had it set up so that her counsellor picked her up at home and took her out for a coke or something when they had their counselling sessions; very humane, very enlightened. But she had nothing else to do but bug Brian now, and he couldn't escape.

Toward the end you could feel death in the air. Brian's breathing was more labored, shallow, rasping. He even ceased being bothered by Babs.

There was one point when I saw him so struggling to breathe that I asked Tanya: "Should I call a nurse?"

She shook her head, fatalistic, resigned. Even if you could prolong the agony a little longer, why?

Finally Tanya had had enough of Babs. Babs was rattling on about "There's this cute guy down at Carter House, Jim Peterson, I really wonder if I should go for him. He's engaged, but I don't know if I can get him 'disengaged,' or however you say it."

"It's late," said Tanya (8:30 — the end of visiting hours, although no one ever threw us out. Tanya was on the staff, after all, and to all intents and purposes I was family), "maybe it's time for you to go."

"Oh, really?!" said Babs.

She knew she was being a pain, very unsuccessfully pretending ingenuousness.

"Yes, I really think it's time to go."

"O.K."

And she was up. She didn't like Tanya much. Babs was the master manipulator, Tanya impossible to manipulate.

Babs had always been a thorn in Brian's side. It had taken him years to really accept the fact that she was an incurable psychotic, and then, even after he had accepted it, he'd never been able to quite cope with it.

Once Babs was gone, Brian brightened up a bit, momentarily revived.

"Listen, after I'm gone, I want the boy to have my books, but you've got to save them for him until he's old enough. And the girls, use your own judgement, all the bronzes from India, the pre-Columbian stuff. I worry about Twyla; she's got so much potential, but to make it in the art-world she's got to learn the ropes. So much of it is marketing. And Amy... there's such a thin line between being a great entertainer and being a whore."

He stopped. Exhausted. A dull yellow-white, like just-cooked spaghetti. Tried to sit up.

"There's a notebook in the drawer..."

"Here?"

I opened the top drawer of the bedside table.

There was a black, perfect-bound notebook in the drawer, the kind Brian over the years had always used to write his novels in.

"That's it. It's the notebook I kept this summer. I want you to have it."

Tanya looked disturbed. She must have known he was keeping a diary. Of course, she is such a private, secretive person. My first thought was, WAS SHE WORRIED ABOUT WHAT HE'D SAID ABOUT HER?

Brian either didn't notice or didn't care about her reaction.

"Do what you want with it. Take it. I want you to have it."

And he thrust it into my hand with a kind of last thrust of energy, and then he was done in, kaput, finished. He lay back and closed his eyes, his breathing like the bellows on an old foot-pumped organ.

"Do you want to hang onto it?" I asked Tanya, handing it over to her.

"No, no," she said, and it was then that I realized that it wasn't fear of what it might say about her that kept her so interested in the diary, but rather the fact that what had been his, whatever he'd written, touched, was precious to her. And I was even a little jealous of that. Ever since Holly had walked out on me, no one had felt that way about me; nor had I been able to feel that way about anyone else.

I took the notebook.

Of course, once I'd transcribed it I gave it back to her. But I had been afraid that if I didn't transcribe it, it was never going to get transcribed. Eventually I hope to go through all the stacks of Brian's unpublished novels and scholarly works and (with Tanya's go-ahead) get them re-typed and resubmitted through workable channels. Brian felt that writing ended when you finished the page; I see the writing itself as only a preliminary stage of marketing.

Later, as I transcribed it, I was somewhat disappointed at the journal. Which, I suppose, is the last thing I should tell anyone who is about to read it.

Only compared to the rest of his work, it seemed much too conventional and sane, none of the shamanistic magic of the poems and novels — as if cancer had drained his divine madness out of him, flattened everything out.

My favorite book of his is the novel IN THE MOUTH OF THE CAT, which is about a Shang dynasty shaman who has come to the New World to the Olmeca-Shang colony in the state of Tabasco, Mexico. It's based on Shang-Olmec motifs in which a human being is portrayed in the mouth of a feline, the feline presumably serving as a kind of "familiar" (if I may borrow a witchcraft term here) to transport the shaman to the center of the world in the middle of a trance.

It's a book full of Amerindian lore and madness. You'd swear that Buckley had been an LSD freak or something — but as far as I know he never took any drugs at all. Maybe smoked a little pot back in the Sixties, but that was it.

VOYAGE TO THE HOUSE OF THE SUN was another favorite of mine, Brian's most fully-realized novel on all counts: plot, characterization and unity.

It's based on the idea that the ruins at Tiahuanaco, Bolivia, once housed the Sun-King/Sun-God of ancient world myth, the Helios and Aeetes of THE ODYSSEY and ARGONAUTICA, the House of the Sun in Amerindian (say Hopi) myth. It was based on an intimate knowledge of the ruins at Tiahuanaco themselves and represents a daring amalgam of myth, legend, folklore and invention.

Brian's best poetry is the same way. Like some lines from "The Dead":

> The last tendrils of weak
> Power
> welling up from the bowels of
> Strength,
> the further down you go, the
> more Power there is, into the
> Realm of the Dead
> (gods),
> break their bones and clay
> food- and drink-
> pots, enter your home through
> false doors,
> on the Day of the Dead
> feed/appease them.

Of course, you have to practically be an anthropologist to understand this sort of thing. It just so happens that this is one of the poems that Brian explained to me.

It's based on his reading of Frazer's work (two volumes, I believe) THE DEAD, *and has to do with the fear of the dead returning to hurt the living. So you break the pots that were left in the graves filled with food and drink for The Dead's journey to the Underworld, you trick The Dead by entering into your house by a false door, so they can't follow you. At the same time you recognize the power of The Dead and try to appease it — like during the Hopi feast of Wuwuchim, the equivalent of our Halloween.*

The final journal lacks this magic element. I would have expected Brian's work to become more preternatural/ritualistic/primitive the closer he got to death himself, but it was exactly the opposite; what happened was that it became flatter (I was going to write bourgeois). Still, it has great value in showing the other, non-primitivistic, non-learned side of Buckley's personality, and, at times, stripped of all its scholarly accretions, I find the prose (and ideas) extremely moving.

But back to Brian's giving me the diary in the first place.

He'd given it to me and fallen asleep as if a huge burden had been lifted off his chest.

Tanya and I sat there in silence for a long time, Tanya looking more like 70 than 40. Brian used to tease her about how she aged as the day went on: "You look about 14 in the morning, by evening it's more like 90."

We were both dozing, half in and half out of the room, when Brian sat up, doubled over, spasmed like a clenching fist, one knee jerking up, opened his eyes wide, his mouth open as if to talk, and then he closed his eyes, collapsed back on the bed. It was over. He was gone.

"It must have been an embolism," said Tanya and pushed the nurse's call button, "we'll find out in the autopsy."
No tears, no breakdown. All very matter of fact.
Of course, that's all she dealt with all day, every day: the mute, inert rubble of death.
She was beyond tears or even despair. What I felt I was picking up was some sort of ancient Portuguese-Brazilian fatalism. His death was her death. It was the other side of Brazil, the non-Black, Portuguese, FADA heritage.
It was something that Brian had always complained about to me: "It's not that she goes up and comes down, none of that manic-depressive penduluming. At the same time it's not really depression either. Depression is the bottom of the bucket, and she's already through the bottom into her own dimension of despair, like she's spent her entire life with her head lowered, waiting for the axe."
I've transcribed the diary.
There were a couple of words here and there I had to guess at, but remained 99.9% on target. Brian always wrote in a scrawl anyhow, and toward the end the scrawl turned into labored, private hieroglyphics caught somewhere between sleeping, waking and death. But by the time I got to the end of the transcription, I felt perfectly at ease with it, inside his head and (if I may say so) inside his very heart. I kept thinking of Keats' last poem to Fanny. How does it go, THIS WHITE HAND REACHES OUT TO YOU FROM THE GRAVE...
So here is the diary.
I think this is exactly what he would have wanted me to do with it.

HOWARD FINE

OCT. 29, 1992
EAST LANSING, MICHIGAN

AN ATTEMPT TO DIAGRAM BRIAN'S FAMILY RELATIONSHIPS

(I hesitate to call it a Family Tree.)

Brian's Father	Brian's Mother
4 sisters:	1 brother: Jake.
1) Daisy ("epileptic" — probably schizophrenic). 2) Babe (married Bill Burns, had 3 children: George, Bob and Barbara). 3) Caroline (unmarried). 4) Rose (married George Avery, had 5 children: Jack, Dave, Dick, Bill and Bessie).	Jake's daughter, Judy, married Gene Pawlowski, had 3 children: Tom, Debbie & Gene Jr.

Brian himself was married 3 times:

I. To Maria del Carmen Robledo. Three children:
1) Margarita
2) Brian Junior
3) Barbara (Babs)

II. To Christine Babcock. Three children:
1) Amy
2) Twyla
3) Chris

III. To Tanya Pessoa. No children.

After Christine divorced Brian, she became a Lesbian and moved in with Mimi.

Brian's best friend was Larry Kopf. His wife, Hilda, was (still is) hospitalized after surgery for brain cancer — a permanent blank.

Larry had (has) a girlfriend named Beth. Larry's children are Lisa, Shari and Jeff.

BRIAN BUCKLEY'S DIARY

FRIDAY, JUNE 2
LARRY KOPF'S PLACE IN BROOKLYN HEIGHTS

Three days with the boy now. Of course, I had to take him to New York. Not to see New York — that wasn't the point. The point was to see me and Larry together, to see what friendship, bonding, affection, my being part of a healthy long-term relationship can mean. The positive back-flow into the rest of your life from long, stable relationships.

Anne, the boarder, is gone. After five years of her in the basement, it's mine again.

I even found one of my old Yardley's lavender colognes in the medicine cabinet.

The boy's asleep on the sofa a few feet away. One overhead (ceiling) light on. It's like the set of *Requiem for a Heavyweight*, you walk out through shadows spotlighted here and there. An old Jimmy Durante exit.

I was so afraid that Christine was going to renege on her promise. She's got all these barriers up. Her being a Lesbian isn't so much instinct as a political platform. Of course, how much of anything we do is instinct and how much is will? I think WILL is the key here. She could just as much will herself back in love with me as will to keep huge distances between us.

What I will seems too trite and conventional — with a touch of Kingdom Come to it. I will us all back together again. I will all our instincts back in place, no dislocations, no willed departures from preprogrammed, genetic, biological normality.

I will Mama Bear and Papa Bear and all the three bear kids all back together under the same roof. And if that means giving Tanya the axe, so be it.

I want us all to be one again. Primitive family unity makes so much sense, Grandma and Grandpa and maybe you bring your bride home. I'm thinking of *The Book of Job* and the Indo-Chinese. For all the negative that comes from closeness, you look up from your deathbed and you're surrounded by faces you've known all your life — you go into the Afterlife accompanied by the trumpets of the past.

Larry over at Beth's tonight. For a moment I was pissed. Our first night in town. He could have stayed here one night. But I didn't say anything. I suppose he only really keeps the house in order to fool his mother-in-law and the head of the family trust company (his wife's cousin) into thinking that, in spite of the fact that his wife is in the hospital dying a long, lingering death of brain cancer and complications, that he's still faithful — whatever that means in the circumstances.

Te absolvo! — that's what I'd like to tell him. *Live!* *L'Chaim.* Hilda doesn't even know who you are anymore, what's the difference what you do?"

But I guess he has pretty much absolved himself.

After Chris went to sleep, I went upstairs and looked around a little. Lisa's room almost unchanged, the closet still full of her clothes, an old Rick Springfield record still on the goddamned record machine. She's only across the river in Manhattan and Larry doesn't see her any more than once or twice a year. Shari's room already turned into a "library" — there must be a million dollars worth of handpainted/lithographed books on birds in there. All traces of her obliterated. And Jeff's room, he still has chess trophies from Yale on the bookcases, the (almost) complete works of Jung and Freud, ties still hanging from the closet door — although he's already been in California now for five years. I could feel his "presence" still humming there, his smell, his ghost.

The past became so real for me upstairs that when I came down, if Hilda had been sitting on the sofa as always, smoking away, with a glass of ginger ale and a package of Pepperidge Farm chocolate chip cookies on the table in front of her, instead of lying dying in a nursing home five blocks away, I wouldn't have been surprised.

I don't want it to ever happen to me with such finality, this diaspora — the total shattering of old villages in the center of my soul.

People laugh at my phone calls, my visits to Kansas City, my letters, presents, all the thousands I spend in air fares every year.

Thank God the boy's here with me.

The pen begins to stray all over the page now. Like a drunk dog. Goddamned cough. Post-nasal drip. Allergies. Maybe I can stop it for the night with a little Nyquil.

JUNE 3
AFTER SIGHTSEEING

Larry lent me his membership cards for the Metropolitan and Brooklyn museums (and Natural History Museum) and today we hit the Met.

Is Chris just a normal eight-year-old twit or another "case" in the family?

I couldn't get him to focus on anything, so I made a deal with him. "Give me fifteen minutes of attention and, god-damit, I'll find you some video games, O.K.?"

That's all he seems to be able to relate to — video games.

Last night, before he went over to Beth's, after Chris had been bugging the both of us all day to go out and find a game arcade somewhere because Larry didn't have any game-system hooked up to his TV, Larry finally told Chris: "In New York we don't have to have video games, we've got reality!"

So we got to the museum, and I went up to the Impressionists.

For me they're all great Buddhas, the closest anyone has gotten to *Samsara* (Enlightenment) among all modern artists. Suzuki on canvas.[1]

Three minutes in front of one of Monet's paintings of the façade of the cathedral at Rouen.

"You get up close, and it's just splotches. It looks like eczema, skin cancer. But then you move back, and it starts to become real. *Trompe l'oeil.* You fool the eye. You think you're seeing reality, only what is reality? What do you/can you really see?

What Monet wanted to do was capture the moment. He did whole series of pictures of this cathedral, pictures of haystacks, morning, noon, evening. Like Whistler's *Fireworks*. Big scandal. "Is this art?" everyone asked. And in terms of what everyone else was doing, it wasn't. He was pushing beyond boundaries/frontiers, trying to make paint really represent the Out There. Although (stepping back and holding the boy's head toward the canvas) in a way he did succeed."

Pissaro's Montmartre Boulevard.

Again back and forth, close up, then distancing. You could practically hear (and smell) the horses, the voices, the shuffling of feet on the pavement. One moment transfixed.

A Van Gogh sunflower.

"I went down to Arles one time," I tell the boy, "Southern France, right in the middle of the summer. And I looked

---

1. Suzuki — One of Brian's favorite authors on Buddhism. [All notes are by the Editor, Howard Fine.]

for Van Gogh's sunflowers and fields, right where he painted them. And they weren't there."

"What do you mean they weren't there?" he asks. I'd finally gotten a hook into him.

"The fields of sunflowers were there, but not *his* fields. They were in Van Gogh's head, in his own personal chemistry. Like he'd take a very ordinary bowl of fruit and turn it into a color whirlpool. Or turn an ordinary sky into snakes of lights."

"And it was all in his head?"

Focusing in now; the pinwheels stop spinning.

"Well, yes and no. When I was down in the Atacama Desert two years ago with Twyla, I'd go out and look up at the night-sky and there weren't even individual stars. It was like I could see them all, star-ropes, star-yarn, you know what I mean? Van Gogh was supposed to be crazy, taking Digitalis. It changed the way he saw things. But who says our 'normal' chemicals make us any closer to what's really out there?"

One more painting. Another Pissaro. Winter afternoon view of the Tuilleries.

I start thinking about my other buddy (in San Francisco), Horse Morse, the sci-fact writer, who at the age of 50 discovered that he'd never been alive and started chasing everything with a Swiss-German, French or Italian accent he could find working in a coffee-bar in San Francisco. No spectacular results, but a little juice flowed and I'd get these endless letters from him opening up inside, defossilizing, the Springtime of the Spirit, middle-aged rebirth, La Vie Bohème, Rudolfo, Mimi. One time I'd answered his newly-kindled sexuality with "We were born in the wrong place in the wrong century. WE are the quintessential Romantics."

"It really captures it, doesn't it? That winter light," I say.

"When will the fifteen minutes be up?" he asks.

"I guess now, maybe," I say.

I'm not making it. I'm too hot, too fast, too self-conscious. Maybe I should just stand and look, let him look, interiorize, Suzuki, coming in and out of Nothingness. I'm never with the kid enough to just silently convey patterns and attitudes, always feel frantic, like I have to make up for lost time.

There was a Goya retrospective going on. I grabbed him by the hand.

"O.K., let's get some ice cream," pretending the Goya retrospective was the way out.

Goyas I'd never thought about much. Goya as court painter. Not the Goyas I loved in the Prado in Madrid, the dying syphilitic madman painting nightmares out of his collective unconsciousness. This was Goya the ass-kisser, like me in the university, I suppose. Neanderthals at court. Or was I being fair to the Neanderthals, who I really believed were much nobler and much more intelligent than anyone (except myself and Charles Olson) had ever imagined?

I thought of Jean Renoir, the film-maker — the painter's son.

I'd known him in California, loved his films, read his book about his father, how he'd cut off all the sharp edges on the furniture and round them down with sandpaper so that the kids wouldn't hurt themselves if they fell.

Going back to my own childhood now, when I was eight years old like Chris... what do I remember?

The first thing that came to mind was climbing up to the top of the Pyramid of the Sun at Teotehuacan outside Mexico City. In the rain no less. No one else around. Years before Mexico had been discovered by tourists at large.

If you abused a child, the abuse charted the course of his whole future. What about this short trip through the world of the Visionaries, even with a guide as stodgy and over-anxious as me?

Out of the museum. Two Dove Bars.

"What about video games?" he asks.

"O.K.," I say. Only where in God's name are there any video-game parlors in Manhattan? In fact are they even feasible/possible?

There's a black man standing under a tree. Mr. Black Vinyl, with a Batman hat on, like he was looking for an angry fix.

"You wouldn't happen to know where there's any video games around town, would you?"

"You asked the right guy, my man — Penn Station."

"Penn Station?"

"That's it."

"Thanks a lot."

"No problem."

And we're off to Penn Station. Batman's Gotham Gothic city.

We find the video games, the boy's happy...

It's funny to see some six-foot-five black guy in black leather, wearing chains around his neck and wrists, right in the middle of Double Dragon. Chris comes up, drops in a quarter, joins in the game — tacit but total acceptance. You don't have to say it, it's there: *Get on board, kid, have some fun.* And then they're allies against The Video Enemy.

I drop a couple dollars. He still wants to play more. I've gotta put a lid on it. Let's try a call to his mother, find some phones, call Kansas City, Twyla answers.

"Hey, babe, howya doin'?"

"Bored out of my skull," she says, "I hate Kansas City."

"Go down to the Art Institute, that's where you belong."

"Yeah, if I could *get* there."

"Go in with your Aunt Clara in the morning, come back with her in the evening."

"It's too far out of her way to pick me up here. And, besides, that'd be a ten-hour day every day, that sounds too much like work."

"Well..."

I'd love to have her back up with me. Is she stable enough to handle it? I wonder.

"Listen, is your mom around? I thought we could get our daily call in...."

"No, she's not here. I don't know where she is."

"O.K., I'll call later. So, besides being bored, what's going on?"

"I'm afraid."

"Of what?"

"Just Out There. Everything."

"Reminds me of Margy Van der Dice out in San Francisco."

The woman who lives with Horse Morse. Twenty-three years since she's been out the front door. Like raging surf, mad dogs, seas of fire and howling winds between her and Out There.

"I'm not crazy!"

"Phobic. You can get 'desensitized,' 'de' and then 're'-conditioned."

"But it takes money."

"Try to find someone, then we can talk about cost."

"Do you really think I need to go through all that?"

"Look, I had padre-confessors, spiritual advisors, years of torture, stuttering, stammering, indecision, three wives, I've been writing it out for decades as a form of auto-psychoanalysis, and even now... Look, my father's sister, Daisy, was in an institution for years, assorted cousins haven't been able to get out of the front door most of their adult lives. We all need help."

"I'll ask Mom."

"I can talk to her about it later too."

"O.K., pal."

"I love you."

"I love you too."

And I hang up, starting to cry. Don't even try to talk; I won't be able to.

The burden she carries with her from our cursed collective past. And my mother always lying, covering up. Her grandmother died, killed by a train, supposedly; I was never supposed to find out about that, but my grandmother was confessional toward the end, and a few things came out. Hit by a train, or suicide? How much can I ever hope to find in old newspaper files from the end of the nineteenth century?

Down to the park a couple of blocks from Larry's place, and then out to the Promenade.

"You wanna see the Statue of Liberty — there it is."

Out right in front of us. And then you let the eye travel right, across Battery Park, and there's the World Trade Center.

"There's King Kong Towers," I say, pointing across the East River.

"Where's Ghost Busters' Headquarters? Can we go there?"

What does he know/care about King Kong?! The instant obsolescence of the pop world.

"It's down on 54th and 3rd Avenue, I think," I answer, "Larry'll probably know the exact address."

As if there really was a Ghost Busters Headquarters. Where do you draw the line between Manhattan as fantasy and Manhattan as fact?

Larry's back at the house at six, we go over to visit Hilda at the Red Hook Nursing Home, this mouldering pile of red brick in the midst of the toughest neighborhood in Brooklyn. He puts his sign in the window — NO RADIO.

Why don't they steal whole cars? Is it too hard to get away with it?

The linoleum is new in the newly-painted (lime-green) corridors. Larry knows patients and nurses alike.

"Where are we going?" asks Chris.

"To see Larry's wife, she's got brain cancer."

She's asleep in her room. Doesn't look bad. In fact looked a lot worse ten years ago when she'd smoke al day and never eat. Now she eats and she's stopped smoking. Her skin... I think of a little pink piglet.

Larry's the one who's grey now, him and his endless flirtation with lung cancer, chain-smoking unfiltered Camels for thirty years. Not that I can talk, me and my goddamned pipe that I never really enjoyed/enjoy. It began, like my horn-rimmed glasses, for appearance's sake (the very model of a modern major professor) and ended up hooking me like a beef carcass on a meat hook. Every night ending up a little sick, nauseated, dizzy, with a stinging red tongue.

Hilda stirs, opens her eyes, Larry bends over her.

"Brian's here with his little son, Chris..."

No recognition, then 'something,' an attempt to speak that comes out URGH, a kind of stammered growl.

"Hilda, hello," I say, "I didn't come a thousand miles for a blank stare." But that's all I get.

She'd been the most brilliant (and vindictive) lawyer I'd ever met. I used to sit in the back of the courtroom when she'd have a juicy murder case. That's what she liked, to shishkebab a particularly vicious killer. "To get back at my father," she'd laugh when I'd question her enthusiasm.

Twenty years of intimacy and now I don't think she even has a hint of who I am. Everything erased, like a blackboard hit with a firehose.

We stay a little longer. Inez, in the bed next to her, talks to me, as always, in Spanish, as always a slight stutter, "*Como está... que hay d-d-de nuevo?*" ("How are you? Wh-Wh-What's new?")

"*Nada, todo viejo.*" ("Nothing, everything old.")

We sit around ten minutes more. Hilda stares at us, we stare at her, Inez stares at all of us. It's a zombie convention. The City Morgue.

And then we go, Larry visibly depressed for a few minutes, until we get on to the Brooklyn Bridge.

"This is Brooklyn Bridge," he tells Christopher. "There's a great poem about this bridge." And he starts quoting/misquoting Hart Crane.

I love the ride across the bridge to Manhattan, the Empire State Building over to the right, the Chrysler Building.

The bridge is metal-grid surfaced. It sings. It really does sing.

Beth lives in a doorman-manned condominium. She's comfortable — I suspect mainly because of Larry. Who really loves her. Which I understand/don't understand. She's not pretty, she's not young, she's not artistic or creative in any big ways, but she's pretend-normality, a pretend-home with a pretend-wife waiting for him.

Her mother lives with her now.

The mother is a bright penny of an 85-year-old woman who graduated from Boston University when it meant something, and taught Italian in the Boston public schools for forty years.

I like the way she talks, the way she looks. Aristocratic, finicky, professorial. Not much of it got passed on to Beth who seems like such a square block of a peasant next to the old lady. Squat and chunky like a touristy Mexican onyx Choc Mool paperweight.

The old lady talks about Puccini, a new production at the Met, defends the Girl of the Golden West.

"Forget the text/libretto, that was what always plagued Puccini — the lack of a decent libretto. Although he wasn't alone with the problem. Look at Tannhäuser!"

Beth is condescending, treats the old lady like a "case." All she can talk about is food.

"I don't know, I just have a taste for Middle Eastern: couscous, humus, falafel..."

"Well, it can be arranged!" says Larry like he was a big fat genie out of a magic lamp.

There's an Algerian place two blocks away. Larry and I go and get big bags of take-out stuff. It's great.

Chris acts like an asshole at times, insists, insists, insists on TV, can't sit still at dinner, and when they do let him loose with the TV, he finds WRESTLING and won't let go.

I know how it is in Kansas City. There's no time for the kid. Christine's too busy playing slave to the Great Dictator, Mimi. But I refuse to say/think anything wrong about his mother. There isn't anything, really. Mimi's the creep. Another Beth, maybe worse. They ought to get together, Beth and Mimi.

I wish I had the boy during the year, but I don't — and have to fit years into months. I was going to write "lifetimes into months."

I feel punk.

It's 2 a.m., Larry drives us home and then goes back to Beth's.

I wish it was exactly like the old days, Hilda still around, going to bed, the kids all asleep, Larry and me sitting around until two or three, going out and walking the dog, talking about life. Then him doping out the next day's races.

Chris asleep on his sofa. I look over at him. He looks like a little old man. And, of course, he'll *be* a little old man and I'll be fifty years dead. How I wish I could hitch my life to his star, not have to get off at all. My Little Prince.

JUNE 4 — SUNDAY

We went to Belmont today with Rich Barth and his son Moss.

I made about twenty bucks on the betting-pool. Of course, Larry's the Big Handicapper in the Sky. The horses saved him during those years between Hilda's first getting cancer and his meeting Beth, when he was treating every woman he met like she was a life-raft and he was drowning.

He knows all the genealogies of all the horses, the stables, the trainers, the times, the track conditions.

You'd hear him say things like "Lucky Jim in the Fifth looks good. From the Lucky Four Stables in Kentucky. A little tendinitis a year ago May, won a couple races in the boondocks, trainer's Joe Wiley, great with turf-racers."

He'd go on. He'd know the great-grandmothers and -grandfathers of every horse on the track, and if they ran well in a South wind and whether planes (from Kennedy) in the distance threw them off their stride.

It was that kind of encyclopedic know-how that saved Larry from blowing out his brains or letting someone else do it for him. Like *Equus* — Horse, be my god!

Chris got bored fast, of course, although I thought it was good for him for a change to get a whiff of cigar smoke and have some clam chowder and bet a couple horses, get a touch of masculine ritual, how it feels to be one of the guys, New York style.

Rick fat and funny as always. Travel business. His son's finishing high school, talking about Engineering at NYU. A little on the Fifi side, but he'll be fine. The apple never falls far from the tree and all that.

Rick lost, of course. That's his ritual, to come in and win hard at first, then lose at the end. That's his role — loser on purpose. We're all stooges, and Larry's the Baron. And Chris the Perpetual Sore Thumb.

Everyone in Kansas City thinks he's a dyslexic, hypertensive nutcase, the guy who'll never turn a screw or finish a computer game, the born loser.

I took him out to the park outside the stands, told him "Stay here!," a thousand other kids twice as wild as him. In fact, here he was low key, for crissake. It's all so relative. I don't know how the chains on the suspended tires and swings and platforms just don't snap. Standing there you're confronted with this giant apocalyptic roar.

Went to get us two ice cream bars, came back, the kid was gone. Started looking through the whole playground, the little boy with the Batman cap. Nowhere to be seen.

My first thought, of course, was that he went off with someone and I'd never see him again.

Found a woman cop.

"I've lost my kid."

"Oh, about thirty get lost every day. What does he look like?"

Big help.

"Like everyone else in this park."

His mother's gonna kill me, I thought, I'm gonna kill myself.

And here he comes with this Latino kid.

"Where have you been, for crissake?"

"My friend and I were just looking for video games."

The Prodigal Son — that which was lost is found.

"Come on, you guys, let me buy you some ice-cream."

More Dove bars. The other little boy distrustful when I asked him where he lived, me thinking maybe Chris could have a friend his own age in New York.

I didn't pursue it, stayed and watched him play for a while, Batman cap, Joker shirt.

I had wanted so much for Chris to meet Menke Katz, the Kaballistic Jewish Wiseman up in Glen Falls. Upper State New York, not too far from Albany. Twenty-one years I've been visiting Larry twice a year, 42 visits to Menke Katz, 42 dinners, 42 afternoons and evenings, and it's as if I'd been his disciple full-time for 42 years — his shadow stretches that heavily across my life.

TALMUD.

I didn't even know what it was when I began. Me, the Irish-Catholic, Mass and Communion every day for 20 years, communing with the Godhead, the Eleusinian Mysteries, but how do you get it to rub off on your everyday life? With Menke everything was practical, applicable.

"How is the wiseman like an olive stone? In order to get oil out of the stone, you have to crush it. In order to get wisdom out of a man, he must be crushed too!"

Which was his verdict on the sea-change I'd gone through in the last few years. I'd been crushed all right, and it was the best thing that had ever happened to me.

The only time I'd ever gone against Menke was when he told me never to forgive Christine for having falsely accused me of sexually molesting Chris. Especially after I told him how she and Mimi had actually made a tape and had taken it to the cops:

CHRISTINE: *Did your father ever put anything in your mouth?*
CHRIS: *Gum, he put gum.*
MIMI: *GUNK? He put GUNK in your mouth?*

"That's horrible," Menke had said, "to use words in that way, premeditated, nothing in anger, but in cold blood."

"Christine's blood has never been too cold," I'd answered, and then switched back away from personalities to abstract ethics: "Only what about Christ and forgiveness, you forgive seven times seven times seventy-seven. The whole basis for your existence is forgiveness."

"And you get crucified! It's a simple equation," he said and then started reconsidering, recomputing. The Old Talmudic/Zen Master.

TALMUD wasn't dry-as-dust laws on tablets but a habit of thinking, discussing, working things out. Like an ethical debate society. That was the whole point of it, a methodology, not dogma. Something alive and flexible.

And I remember, a week later he'd called me in Michigan.

"Maybe you're right, if you don't forgive, it's true, the lamb will never lie down with the lion, the Jew and the Arab will never sit down to the feast together. Maybe the philosophy of never forgiveness is a little outmoded. Jesus was the first reformed Jew, that's what he was, just a couple thousand years too early."

But I'm missing the essence of Katz. The craggy, old, wild-eyed enthusiast, essentially poor, but you never thought that, he and his wife living on her pension in a little home up in the mountains. He'd never "worked" for the last 40 years, really, just read TALMUD and KABALLAH, meditated, read, wrote poetry and Biblical commentary. It was an inward, contemplative life, a little hut up on top of the mountain behind his house, that the wind blew away: "The wind ate it up. You should never get the wind mad at you."

Katz's essence is like Buber talking against Buddhism:

> If I lived a thousand lives, if reincarnation were true, instead of trying to escape from those thousand lives like the Buddha, I would grasp them to me and live them all as totally as I could...

The essence of Katz is that — you turn up the Life Thermostat. You think more, you feel more. You feel with your mind. It's Pater's burning with a .hard gemlike flame, with an ancient Middle-Eastern mystical dimension.

What he's really saying all the time is *be here, turn up the moment, burn it away without a trace.*

That's what I've gotten from him, not the cold tomb Cisternian embalming of my youth, but the dove descending and breaking the air every minute after minute, pentecostal tongues of flames always flickering on the tops of our everyday heads.

Amen.

But I guess we're not going to make it to Menke's this time. No time. Pressure from Beth. I guess Larry doesn't take Beth with him when he goes to visit Menke, which, I imagine, is Beth's choice. For her all religion is bullshit. She's not really Catholic, not really anything. I remember one night making fun of my taking Menke seriously. "I'm an Egg-nostic, I believe the universe hatched out of a giant cosmic egg."

Ha, ha, ha, ha.

So much for Menke, KABALLAH, TALMUD — and Jesus, the First Reformed Rabbi.

Tomorrow the Brooklyn Museum.

Amen.

JUNE 5TH — MONDAY
№ MUMMIES

The Brooklyn Museum would have been a total failure if it hadn't been for the U.S. Latino exhibit.

I always like to immerse myself in the Egyptian stuff, the mystery of pre-dynastic Gerzean pots, the Nagada culture. I remember when I first saw Nagada stuff in an exhibit in Spain (Valencia), I blew my lid. The Amerindian connections were so obvious. And later, when I came across the Egyptian references to the Land of the Setting Sun, the Land of the Lake and the Peak in the West — the Urani (?) people. I forget the exact word. But it clicked. Urani... and then you go across the ocean and you find the Uros living on Lake Titicaca in Bolivia, under the shadow of Mount Illimani, the Peak in the West.

There have even been statues of the Egyptian childbirth god, Bes, found in Mexico.

I remember seeing a statue of Bes in a shop near the British Museum, unlabelled, going in and asking: "How much is the statue of Bes in the window?" And the woman working there kind of astounded: "There's not one person in a million who would know that name." I guess I was that one person in a million. Which is why I wish people wouldn't take my identifications, my intuitions, my drawing of lines between Culture A and Culture B so lightly.

Be that as it may, for all my enthusiasm, Chris couldn't have cared less about the Egyptian stuff.

No awe.

All he wanted to see was a mummy. No sarcophagi, bowls, canopic jars, statues — a mummy! Only there weren't any.

And then we chanced on this exhibit of Latino art in the U.S., and Chris got turned on. Bigger-than-life figures in a saloon, huge wild dogs, a cat-woman whore named Mariposa (Butterfly). The whole thing pulsated with minority, primitive-roots power. This wasn't the starched and ironed-our Middle Class, but LA RAZA!

One guy standing puzzled in front of a Franciscan-altar kind of construction.

"That's a symbol of St. Francis of Assisi," I said, "see the stigmata?" Four bloody splotches on the front side of the altar.

"Thanks," he said.

Getting points for myself in Chris's eyes — functioning (mainly) as the real me.

I know what a total antiquarian, dust-covered, mummified nerd I am. I've spent my whole life in concert halls, practice rooms, art studios, art museums, in libraries, at a type-writer/word-processor, playing violin and piano and bassoon, singing the role of Sarastro, the high priest in *The Magic Flute* at age 12. Strange life, strange gods, strange altars. But it almost has been a religion for me. I feel like a Keeper of the Sacred Seal, a High Priest of Isis, the librarian/art cri-tic/poet/novelist/dreamer. The boy didn't get a baseball/foot-ball-fan father, he got me — and as snobby as it may seem, that's the religion I proclaim and what I want to pass on, a kind of latter-day Epicurianism in the midst of all this contem-porary Yahooism. A sensitivity to the Now, the Now of things, the Now of other peoples' feelings.

After the museum, on purpose I walk a block over to the Grand Army Plaza, avoid the subway, catch a bus, have about five minutes looking up at the magnificent green oxidized figures on top of the triumphal arch.

"What's all that about?" asks Chris, impressed by the magnitude of the arch.

"Civil-War monument," I answer him.

It reminds me of the Arche de Triomphe in Brussels... or in Paris.

He looks up.

"What war was that?" he asks.

"Between the North and the South, over slavery," I answer, referencing back to the Gettysburg Address.

He looks impressed and then starts playing with a Batman figure I'd gotten him in the Detroit airport. But the "over slavery" hovers in the air, especially when we get on the bus to Flatbush and we're the only, the absolutely only whites. It's not something you see in East Lansing or Kansas City, this total segregation/separation.

Destination — Brooklyn College.

I'd called Jackie Eubanks up the night before.

Old friend. Acquisitions librarian, radical free-speech activist.

Jackie and I look like twins — except that she has a permanent. In fact, two weeks ago at the COSMEP convention at the Roosevelt Hotel, she walked into the bar and Repasky, one of my old students from Michigan (now in architecture at Cooper Union), thought it was me in drag.

Same Middle-European genetic stock.

Funny life.

Brooklyn College a kind of fake oasis straining to be artsy and techy and bright and enlightened in the middle of tough-shit disenfranchised Flatbush. Sometimes you wonder how the Republic survives in the midst of so many angry outsiders.

Works in this funny little office right in the middle of the
bowels of the library.

Big moon Middle-European face.

"Gee, I'm glad to see you!"

She's been so great to me over the last five trial-years
(trial as in olive seed crushed for oil, man crushed for
wisdom). First Twyla, when we were on the way to Chile via
New York. I remember she took us out to this Swiss-Italian
restaurant (The Dancing Bear?). The bill came to $60.00 and
she wouldn't (but wouldn't!) let me pay anything. Then Amy
last winter. Again out to dinner. And again on her. Like
Larry giving Amy and me his tickets to an Alvin Ailey dance
concert and the New York Philharmonic. It's like all doors
have been opening for me since I descended into Hell and
resurrected, like I am in the final chapter of JOB now, the
part where Job's children and his children's children surround
him and he has more sheep than anyone else in Israel.

We go over to Jackie's place, about two blocks away,
some black kids appear, they start putting away the kitchen
things that are all over the stove and counter. Back into the
shelves.

"I just painted everything. These are my helpers."

Over the years she'd become a kind of den mother for
the fatherless and/or motherless kids in the neighborhood.
She used to be a Lesbian, then she was all into rough and
tough truck-drivers, now she was the local Great Earth
Mother, Great Goddess — and I guess I'm one of her devo-
tees.

So much between us now. How "love" comes and goes
and comes again, like the seasons, cold waves, warm waves,
the jet-stream dipping down, arching up, totally unpredictable.

Jackie gave me a big drink, rum and coke. I didn't even
notice the proportions of coke and rum, just drank it down,

and before I knew it, there I was — out. She let me sleep, and I slept for a couple hours. When I woke up, Chris and the other kids were sitting in front of the TV watching *Mad Max*, and Jackie was hovering over me, concerned.

"Are you O.K.?"

"What do you mean?"

"I mean are you O.K.? You look, I don't know... are you losing weight or something?"

I automatically reach up and feel my cheeks. The Magyar cheekbones.

"I don't think so, I've just got this cough, that's all."

"O.K."

She's not convinced.

"So how's *Mad Max*?" I ask the kids.

"Not so great," says one of the little black boys, sensitive-looking, big, soft sensitive eyes, lots of expression, "it takes him too long to get mad."

"Come on, I wanna take you guys out to eat," says Jackie.

"Not again!" I protest.

"I mean it. There's this great buffet place..."

And she insists, marches us a few blocks down, right through the decaying heart of Flatbush to this great buffet place. And when it comes time to pay, I pull my (really Tanya's) Visa out like a quick draw.

"Come on!"

"You wanna fight me right now?"

"Not really."

And she pays with her American-Express Card, we settle down, still the sole whites among the soul-people.

"Thanks a lot," I say.

"Be graceful about it," she smiles, "you know how I feel about you and what you're doing..."

I don't even ask her what I'm doing — although I guess I know.

I've become a Katzian, grab onto it — H'ai! Life! Give. Burn yourself out. That's the way Katz was with his own son, spent endless hours with the boy when he was growing up, always speaking Yiddish to him, never a word of English. Some mad talmudic trick of immersing yourself in the *ser* and *estar* of the Other — and now the ex-boy is head of the Yiddish program at Oxford University.

And the irony is that ten years ago, Jackie was my enemy. I remember her, time after time, convention after convention, the ABA, the ALA, COSMEP, she'd always be ragging on me for one thing or another.[2] And then the so-called, self-proclaimed Lesbian started talking about getting it on with black truck-drivers — the "real" her. I just figured that under all the self-defining labels, she was trying to reach a definition of her Self that transcended labels. Like Christine, in a way. If she could just take that amorphous (polymorphous) kingdom within herself and stop trying to label it with something out of the inherently vague label-choices of modern psychology.

But, again, over the years my tactic had been — you don't program me by how you are to me, I'll be the way I want to you, independent of how you are to me. So I'd always been good back to her bad.

We must have been in the restaurant more than an hour. And Chris, I don't know, all the time listening, eating, looking around, throwing in his two cents from time to time.

---

2. ABA = American Booksellers Association, ALA = American Library Association, COSMEP = The Committee of Small Magazine Editors and Publishers/The International Organization of Independent Publishers.

There were deaths and suicides to catch up on, Bill Ryan over the cliffs at Monterrey, Todd Lawson dead of AIDS.

And then back to Brooklyn Heights, Larry (unexpectedly) there.

"Beth's mother fell down this afternoon. Beth just didn't want anyone around."

Chris watching TV. Amazing that Larry doesn't have cable. But Chris found some wrestling and Larry and I sat and talked in the dining room.

"At least Beth doesn't talk any more about having a kid, me divorcing Hilda. All that crap. She's become a realist."

"And if she hadn't?"

"Remember last year, we actually 'broke up.' I wasn't fooling around..."

And he wasn't. Beth had made her play for everything head-on. Not that she'd changed ultimate purposes now, just tactics, from Rock to Cloud. I figured she'd end up with the whole pot eventually anyhow.

He was always complaining to me on the phone when I was back in Michigan: "She's so demanding. She wanted it once at midnight, then again at five a.m., then again at nine. But I managed somehow, don't ask me how."

Always tired out, him and his overweight and diabetes. I always wondered how the will read now, how much she'd already gotten staked out for herself.

It was great just to be there gabbing with him. White hair and beard. Like Jeremiah, something out of a Blake lithograph. God the Father.

It was funny to be talking about divorce and kids and sex and all of that, when both of us were so close to the End. "T-t-that's all folks!" Like we were in our twenties, just beginning, instead of pushing our sixties.

JUNE 6TH — TUESDAY
MY LITTLE PRINCE

C hris happy to go to Penn Station again. We were on our way to Lynne Savitt's, but he would have been just as happy to have stayed there all day on the video games.

Maybe I just lack imagination. I can project myself into Siegfried killing Fafner, but can't make it (really!) into that tiny screen to fight monsters and demons.

We really have become totally dependent on screens, haven't we, video-gamers, computers, TV. Like just before we left Michigan we went to visit Tebida in his new house. Parents from Uganda. One generation back and they were on the Ugandan high plateau. Now Tebida, instead of going out into the pool or over to the school basketball courts, was spending summer in front of the TV, playing video basketball.

It's as if the whole country really was on the threshold of inner space exploration, the dream of the man-electronic splice, as if we were all destined to be robo-cops or robo-robbers, robo-pilots, robo-writers, robo-mystics, robo-prophets.

Here I am on a sofa in the basement of a house in Brooklyn Heights (Larry stirring upstairs, time to turn in, enough deep meditation on the nags for today) writing in my notebook with a fuchsia Flair pen, just one step away from Neanderthal eloquence, and all the rest of the world's gone electronic...

Anyhow, we spent an hour playing videos in Penn Station, then went down and got on the Long Island railroad out to Savitt's, got off the train, made a call and she was there in five minutes.

Middle-class neighborhood. House had belonged to an Italian family, all the walls carpeted, big pool, Lynne looking great except for a bandaged arm.

"Just another tumor. The one of my face ten years ago was malignant, this one was benign."

"What tumor on your face?"

She points to an area under her eye.

"You heal well, I can't see anything."

And I couldn't.

Her daughter's there. The diabetic. First time I've met her. And Lynne's latest husband, this wall-eyed walrusy-looking guy with a big smile. Sanitation engineer. I guess I can figure out what that means. Husband number five, I think.

I'm publishing a book of her dream-poems. Although she has remained relatively unknown, I think she's as powerful as Bukowski, Lifshin, Todd Moore. The main thing about her is feeling. Not very interested in making it big like the rest of them.

Again it's like being with Jackie, this sense of long stretches of time shared, our personal histories twined together; that's all that seems to count for me. I'm ashamed to write it down, but that's the way it is.

How many years, conventions, readings, evenings, letters? She pulls out volumes of photos that go way back. There we are in Berkeley, Lennox, Massachusetts, a party at Charles Hasseloff's back 15 years, her next to Richard Kostelanetz, me next to Dick Higgins.

"It's scary," I say. "I was just getting warmed up, and now it's the last lap."

"I don't care," she says, "I don't even mind the wrinkles and the scars. Just to be here, just to *be*."

She's got a shishkebab barbecue going. A little whiskey on the rocks. Very little for me. I don't want to conk out again. Chris swims in the pool. I watch him and imagine him swimming one length of the pool and turning from 8 to 18.

He's such a nice guy. Straight. My father was a straight nice guy too — that's what I want him to be like. I keep thinking/rethinking that I want to go with the boy through life and not get dumped off. My father died at 75, my uncle (mother's brother) died at 80, my mother's 85, her mother died at 93. I may have 20 years more, a chance to see the boy at 28, live to see a son of his eight-years old. Wouldn't that be something!

I confide in Lynne all my obsessiveness with "passing things on" to the boy.

"Don't worry, he's already your image. I've never seen a kid give himself the way he does. He's all emotion. Very sensitive, the rest comes later, the scholarliness, books, all of that."

Lynne's daughter has to leave, Lynne reads a little poetry, talks a little about her other four husbands, while George smiles on. I keep sipping whatever it is I'm sipping. The afternoon slips away.

Who's counting days? I'm counting hours! Another hour of video games in Penn Station on the way back. We're home by nine, walk out and see the Statue of Liberty again, then home, a nice bath, without TV.

The kid wants me to sleep right next to him every night. Of course, I can't sleep with anyone. Raised in a room and a bed by myself. So I fake it out, tell a little bit of *The Odyssey* to him, the Circe episode, drawing a little from the Mandan-Hidatsa version, so that Circe becomes Old-Woman-Who-Never-Dies, Aeolus becomes Old Windbag Man. The Mandan-Hidatsa version is a lot more vivid than Homer.

He lies in my arms.

I fought (passively, like Gandhi, like the Buddha) three years for this. I can't keep from crying. Nor do I try.

"I love you so much," I tell him, "you're my Little Prince, Little Lord Ahau, like the Ahus on Easter Island, Prince of the Solstice, Morning Star..." [3]

He goes to sleep. I sleep a while, then disentangle myself from him, go over to my own sofa and this journal on the edge of total blackout. Journey to the end of night.

JUNE 7TH — WEDNESDAY

Larry insisted this morning that I take Chris to the Natural History Museum/Planetarium.

So I did — with plans to meet him at the office in the afternoon. Dinner at Beth's again.

The Planetarium show was all about Mars. I kept thinking of when the boy was up at Easter, I'd turn the car radio dial to between stations and tell him: "Listen to that, Martian-talk, they've run out of water and are planning to invade Earth."

"That's just static," he'd say, but I'd keep it up every day. And then I saw an announcement in the paper that they were going to do a new version of Wells's *War of the Worlds* on the university FM station, so I had the boy in my room with the radio on WKAR when they interrupted the music and started in on the reports about strange astronomical observations on the surface of Mars. It wasn't too long, though, before he figured out it was a radio-play.

The next day I took him to the planetarium at the university and when we were coming into the auditorium I told

---

3. A reference to the Maya *Popul Vuh.*

him: "This is a spaceship." We're going on the Mars Mission."
We sat down in our chairs (which were tilt-backs so you
could look up at the ceiling — a slight subliminal suggestion of
airplane seats?) and the poor kid went berserk, started
screaming, wanted to get out. A real panic-reaction. I took
him out, told him I was just kidding and he was O.K. Now
here we go again. No problem this time.

I forget about all the panic-genes on the family DNA, like
flawed pearls. But at least the kids are interesting, vital,
perpetual dawn-suns always rising.

After the show at the Planetarium this time (bringing it
back to the present), we went through the museum, saw the
dioramas, the history of material culture (artifacts) which I
found particularly interesting, especially a Sumerian bearded
statue with a hole in its head (for a candle or — more likely
— incense... even oil to turn it into an oil-lamp) that func-
tionally/iconographically was the same as the New World
figure of the Old Fire God, although a lot less vigorous than,
say, its Zapotec equivalents.

Chris, of course, couldn't have cared less, so I took him
down by Larry's office near City Hall, and we went to all the
job-lot places, Batman figures, games, clothes, whatever he
wanted, bought a cassette-player/radio and some tapes.
Dvořak's 8th, Shostakovich's 7th (the Leningrad), Rachmaninoff's *Rhapsody on a Theme by Paganini*, started playing the
tapes in my pocket when we were on the street between
Weber's and The Pushcart Emporium and Dr. Schlock's, just
a little background music, and then a little background on the
siege of Leningrad, the different themes. I even wrote a
snippet of Rachmaninoff down on a paper bag:

Which didn't mean anything to him as musical notation, but did mean that you could write down musical speech with notes the same way you could write down words with letters. And that it wasn't something inaccessible, but if I could do it on a street in Manhattan, he could do it too — anywhere. It was just a question of time/wanting to learn.

Then down to Nassau St. I got Tanya some spider-web tights just for fun, our monthly hormone-peak one-shot orgy.

Over to the other Pushcart Emporium on Nassau, all the time Shostakovich playing on, the Second World War replayed in the midst of endless rap-crap.

I began violin at age five on a three-quarter size violin (my father was an ex-violinist pushed into Medicine by my M.D.-mad mother), then composition, then opera, The All Children's Grand Opera, Zerlina Muhlman Metzger, who (out of Mahler's Vienna) really changed my whole aesthetic perception of the world, my whole life. There was some message about art/music and sanity — and sanctity. Evil was disorder, art always striving toward, often conterminous with, spiritual order. Can the great artist be evil or doesn't he have to be some sort of prophetic holyman? Artist as modern-day shaman. That's what we want from Monet or Renoir or Rachmaninoff, their holy vision of reality.

Got to Larry's office about 3:30, Sidney Bernard there, as always, Tom Tolney, retired ex-editor-in-chief and current editor-in-chief.

Sidney, as always, eating grapes and yogurt. Comes on strong.

"Brian, how the fuck are ya?"

The old pro. I put him in a class with my old friends Nelson Algren and James T. Farrell, the deadly-serious writer, word-jeweller.

"Pretty good, how about yourself?"

"Just putting together a book of my 1960's pieces. If I can only find a publisher."

"If I had any money I'd bring it out myself."

"I'll find somebody, I always do." Pauses, looks at me more circumspectly: "Are you O.K., pal, you look like you've lost some weight."

"A summer cold, that's all. This is the Kid."

Christopher grinning a gap-toothed grin, looking around, the walls covered with pictures, a computer in the art-room.

Larry's been on the phone in the main office. Now that's over, he comes in.

"You wanna play Ms. Pac-Secretary?" he asks Chris.

"Yeah!"

Any dot moving on any screen and the kid's at home. Larry turns on the system and the kid settles into some serious Pac-Secretarying. Of course, that's concentration/genius that's transferrable to other fields. Again Time. Wasn't I just where he was when I was eight? Of course, I was thrust into so much serious stuff. His mother's more "normal" in that sense; my mother always acted like there was going to be the Big Cultural Literacy Test next week, and if you didn't pass, you got shipped back to Czechoslovakia.

"So how was the planetarium?" Larry asks me.

"Great. More Mars trips."

Larry laughs. He knows all about the debacle over Easter.

Phone rings, Larry goes back into the main office.

"It's hard to imagine that in six months someone else'll be in this office, after us being here for 20 years," says Sidney, Tom just edging in.

"I guess he has no choice."

"Whatever happened to the money?" I ask. I'm not going to ask Larry. These guys see him every day all day, I'm just a visitor from Planet X.

"Well..." Tom has plenty to say but can't say it.

"A pile goes to the nursing home," says Syd.

How many millions were/are there, after all?

Larry off the phone, back in with us.

"Why don't you take a look at the review pile," he tells me, leading me back into the main office.

I've been the Chief Reviewer for *Head* magazine for the last 15 years.

There's a huge pile of unwrapped books and books still in bags and packages. I start to choose a few things. If he doesn't want the reviews for *Head* I'll place them elsewhere.

"Love among the ruins," says Larry, looking nostalgically around, as if he's afraid he's going to forget the twenty years of literary commando warfare he's waged against the Establishment from these offices.

As Chris beeps eternally on.

IN THE BEGINNING WAS THE BEEP,
AND THE BEEP WAS GOD...

JUNE 8TH —
DEBUSSY & RACHMANINOFF

Woke up this morning toppled over on my sofa, pen and notebook fallen on the floor. Last night I told myself I'd just close my eyes a moment, and that was it for the night.

Felt spacey. I want to say "global," floating, like a cottonwood wisp, the spacey biliousness of Debussy's *Nuages...*

I don't know what's wrong with me. I've stopped smoking altogether now, don't even want to think about pipes and tobacco. Asked Tanya on the phone last night what she thinks, but she's the Sphinx. A lot better on autopsies than living people.

"Come on, I know you're thinking something."

"Maybe we should take some X-rays when you get back," she said.

She's a good diagnostician, but I've been there and back too. Mixture 79 and a thousand other mixtures, whole armies of pipes I've burned my way through. And the irony is that it all began as Showbiz, Goodbye Mr. Chips, Sherlock Holmes. The tweeds and the pipe and the professorial horn-rimmed glasses. You begin with an outline and then press the FILL button and it all fills in. With concrete.

Sotheby's this afternoon. Never had been there before. Larry's collecting African pieces. They're all over the house, but today it was $600.00 for a "wax painting" by E.E. Cummings. Very art deco, woman walking a dog in a park, kind of greeting-card Cubism, with no disrespect for Cummings who, after all (The Enormous Room), began life as a painter anyhow. Although I don't really understand Larry's fascination with Cummings. With Audubon and the other bird-artists, African art, O.K., but you'd think Larry would go more for men and art of POWER, not some cutesy-pooh like Cummings...

Other items on auction were some letters by Michelangelo, a holograph score of Debussy's *Three Nocturnes* that I would loved to have bought. *Nuages, Fêtes, Sirens* (as in sea, not cops).

Chris got bored so I took him around the galleries. Russian icons in the basement, a whole collection of Hollywood memorabilia, the Tin Woodman's outfit from the original *Wizard of Oz*, original celluloid prints from Disney classics like *Snow White*...

Then dinner with Beth at a Japanese restaurant, coffee back at her place. Larry stayed there and we took a cab back to Brooklyn Heights. I wanted to pay for it, but he wouldn't let me.

Back to the haunted house. As we were going in (still a dusting of light in the sky) we ran into the daughter of the woman next door — Jillian.

Hadn't seen her for years. Father just dead (from cancer, as a matter of fact) a couple of years, her mother probably very well taken care of (he'd been on Wall Street) — he'd always looked like the incarnation of the Bean Catalogue. He'd had somewhat tan skin but nothing at all to do with the All-American view of rap-crap-crack-blues-bad-news BLACK, had been a kind of dusty-looking New England Brahman Sir Laurence Olivier. Mother ironically now involved with some foundation distributing African films in the U.S. and Europe.

"How you doing, Jillian?"

"Great, how about yourself?"

"Just visiting Larry."

"Does he live there any more? I haven't seen him around."

"Well, he's got a girlfriend..."

"Do tell!"

"Of course I was always hoping that he and your mother..."

"That always remained a possibility. Maybe it still does, I don't know."

"This looks pretty serious."

"How's Hilda doing?"

"She doesn't know who she is or who anyone else is, but she'll probably outlive us all. They got the cancer out.

Then came the strokes. But she looks good. She doesn't know who she is, but she's looking good."

Chris and I go inside, the place hissing with ghosts. I can still hear Hilda (after the first surgery, before the radiation treatments) telling me "Get up and open the door, Sharon's home!"

Sharon was away at boarding school, still a week before Christmas holidays.

"What do you hear?" I'd ask her.

"She's with friends; they're singing Christmas carols."

Nothing there, but I'd get up anyhow, just to shut her up. Look out the door. Of course there was nothing/nobody there.

That was a long time ago, while Hilda was still reacting, even if it was only to voices in her own head. While she could still talk, still knew my face and name. And the kids were there, the house was alive. I was kind of (distantly) in love with Lisa when she started pushing 17, 18, thin, all this romantic cape of long, wispy hair.

You meet someone with twelve million in the bank and at first you think they'd got it made. In fact they did. I'd go up to their island in Maine for a month, it'd be day and night of FAMILY, FAMILY, FAMILY, play cards, talk, walk around on the beach, explore the island, eat, barbecue. I, with my archaeologist's eye, found two old house-sites dating back maybe a hundred and fifty years. It was easy enough. Two walls (no matter how overgrown with moss) converging. Three old trees in a straight, very straight, row. And then you start digging. They thought I was a magician, and I thought they were a textbook perfect family. Hilda treated me like family — better than family. She didn't like anyone else, but she always liked me.

She was out of that magic Jewish Twilight of the Hapsburg Empire. Her father had made a fortune in Czechoslovakia.

Chris wanted to watch TV. O.K., I found a Japanese station, a Spanish station.

Sometimes I think I should speak to him only in Portuguese or Spanish, give him what Menke Katz gave his son — a whole identity (career) just by talking to him full-time in Yiddish.

Gave what you can, what you are.

Then a bath.

Some Rachmaninoff, cassette player hanging on the towel rack.

I've got a keyboard waiting for me back in Michigan. I want to work from heard music, figure out the notation myself, and then teach him to play what I've transcribed. Heard, written, re-heard. Take the mystery out of it. Like Mrs. Metzger taking a whole orchestral score of, say, *Carmen*, and playing it like a piano version.

When I was Chris's age I had an orchestral seating-diagram on the wall of my room, records, these little miniature scores of Beethoven's symphonies. I wanted to be a conductor, but my father had other plans for me — to be a doctor. Which I didn't become either. Left Medicine at 23 to go into writing, and I've done it, goddamit, even if next to nothing's published. Feeling the Rachmaninoff sing through me, crying when we got to:

Two years ago, when I thought I'd never see him, that just maybe his mother, in all her destructive fervor, would pull a disappearing act, I went through the whole Ring Cycle, played all the records, edited, condensed, added voice-over commentary, so he had the whole thing, from the birth of Siegfried to the destruction of Valhalla in, what was it, seven or eight 90-minute cassettes.

The Ring is very special for me. Heroes are very special for me. I was never made for the how-to-succeed-in-business-without-really-trying world.   More at home Rhine-journeying, dragon-slaying, Brunhilde-rescuing.   *Ein Helden-leben.*[4] I should have been a musician like Von Karajan. Full-time. Never come down.

I feel so frail tonight. More like November than June. Leave tomorrow afternoon. Have to get back to Michigan for Margarita's wedding. Really getting more vague, distant. Like I'm floating away from it, it's floating away from me.

JUNE 9, FRIDAY
ON THE PLANE TO DETROIT

Writing this on the plane, the boy next to me asleep. Two hours late. Tanya going to be a case waiting for us all those hours. It was such a short visit. Larry did the impossible and drove us to JFK, got out, we had lunch together.

"I really hate to see you go. When will you be back?"
"Probably not until Christmas."

---

4. *Ein Heldenleben* ("A Hero's Life") — a tone poem by Richard Strauss which is intentionally sarcastic and ironic about heroes.

"Good luck with your mother," he said as he left, and we had three hours of video games and screwing around. Chris is so hyper, but I don't get bothered the way I used to. Kids are kids, Jesus! Not Genghis Khans.

My mother arrives tonight in Detroit.

We're supposed to all meet in the airport, my mother from California, Amy from Kansas City. Now we're two hours late. Weather, I don't know, summer storms. I can just hear my mother, "Why didn't you just skip that silly trip to New York. I haven't been in Michigan for twenty years. I'm 86 years old, don't you think I have any feelings?"

The Via Dolorosa begins again, another crucifixion, only it's getting harder and harder for me to resurrect. All you want is a sweet old lady mother — and what you get is Fafner in drag.

WEDNESDAY, JUNE 14
MONSTER MOM

My mother left for California this afternoon. *Deo gratias, hallelujah.* Haven't had a chance to write a word the whole time she was here.

Attention! Attention! Attention! Frontstage center Medea full-time.

Margarita was married in a beautiful little chapel close to Detroit. Attached to some sort of monastery. Amy gorgeous as always. The modelling school shows. Says she may be coming up to MSU for school in the Fall, just two more high school courses (correspondence — which I always thought was the ultimate cowardice, withdrawal) to finish.

Margarita looked like a model herself. Twenty-nine. Looked nothing like the computer nerd she really is. The only one in the family with my blue eyes, ironic seeing that her mother is 99.9% Bolivian Indian, the other .1% Austro-Hungarian. Which is where the blue-eye gene must have come from, right out of Prague or Budapest.

Maria del Carmen herself looked great, considering her age, weight and general dourness. One thing I've never regretted is walking out on her 20 years ago to marry Christine. Twyla didn't/couldn't come. I offered to pay her way, but I can't even imagine her getting to the airport, getting on a plane. That would be like Emily Dickinson on Mars.

It gets so complicated, first and third wives, the bride from the first marriage, two kids from the second marriage there. Babs, all 300 pounds of her, actually bathed, put on makeup, shaved her legs, and hardly acted psychotic at all. It's funny to see her in all her glorious bulk next to her shrunken little mother — both with matching moon faces.

The little chapel looked very medieval, like a side-chapel at All Souls, Oxford — or Canterbury Cathedral.

My mother bitched at length to the usher that the bride's family should be seated on the right and not on the left, the way he was seating us — after the whole church was already filled up with everyone on the "wrong" (according to her) side. Loud enough for everyone to hear.

And she finally accepted the "wrong" side anyhow, and the priest came out — a comic little Scotchman — and asked the congregation, "Are you guys happy?"

"GUYS?!" said Mom, again loud enough for everyone (including the priest) to hear her. Always on stage.

A hundred heads turned our way.

Then at the reception, Maria del Carmen was supposed to sit with me, Mom and the other kids, but refused, so there were two seats empty, and one of the bride's best friends,

Gloria, her Ecuadorian archaeologist husband and their two kids, were looking for a place and I invited them to sit down.

I introduced them and, naturally, Pepe and I started talking about archaeology — in Spanish. He's working on Olmec-Maya connections at the earliest Maya levels. And I've spent half my adult life in the Andes and Spain, visiting sites, reading the *cronistas*, collecting pre-Columbian ceramics. And for the next two days all I heard from Mom was: "To sit down and speak Spanish. Ignorance! That table was the bride's parents' table. And to bring two little brats to a wedding!"

Isn't that what weddings are all about? And besides, Gloria is Margarita's best friend, Gloria's mother is one of my best friends, Pepe is a professor at the same university where I teach — what's the point?

Tanya looked like she'd stepped right out of Eric Rohmer, Amy was an exploding white chiffon delight, Chris played beautifully with the little kids. *Papacito!* Adumbrations of the future.

My mother even complained about the place where the reception was held.

"What can I tell my friends; it wasn't a country club or even a hotel..."

"It's a wedding-convention center. I thought it was great. Perfect!"

What friends is she talking about? Fellow inmates in the nursing home. Arrgh! Perspective! The long view!

I put her in the Kellogg Center, avoided her as much as I could, gave her long mornings and nap-time after lunch, and then early to bed — but there were still loads and loads of spiny, burning hours.

Babs lives in her mother's basement, gets a monthly stipend from the mental health system, looked great for the wedding, and then the next day reverted back to second-hand, Goodwill-Salvation Army undersized men's shirts and pants, kind of the classic hobo look, stopped washing, no more makeup, started dropping in on my mother at the Kellogg Center every morning for breakfast.

> MOM: I wish you'd stop her coming over to see me in the mornings. I'm so ashamed. She smells. And those clothes! Why don't you buy her any clothes?
> ME: I do.
> MOM: Well, why doesn't she wear them?
> ME: She's crazy.
> MOM: All those abortions.
> ME: Two. And what if they were teenagers now, who'd take care of them — you? She's crazy. When she's off her drugs, she hears voices. They keep telling her to jump, 'Do it!'' She's totally wacko!
> MOM: You don't know that.
> ME: She says she hears them — that's enough for me. Not that it's that unexpected. I've been told that it's genetic, passed through the male to the female.
> MOM: There have never been any mental problems in our family.
> ME: What about Aunt Daisy? She died in Dixon. I saw her there. You took me there to see her.
> MOM (agitated, like a crow about to take flight): I've never been to Dixon in my life. She lived with a family on the Chicago South Side the whole time you were growing up. I used to always bring her clothes.

We're sitting in the lobby of the Kellogg Center. I excuse myself, "I've got to go to the John," go down to the end of the hall, call my cousin George at his pen company in Chicago.

ME: Hey, George, my mom's here for Margarita's wedding. She's just told me that our Aunt Daisy spent most of her life with a family on the Chicago South Side and she didn't die in Dixon.
GEORGE: Right on both counts. She died in the Illinois State Mental Hospital in Elgin, and she spent most of her life in private homes paid for — and paid very little — by Aunt Caroline...
ME: O.K., pal, thanks. Wish me luck!

And I go back to Mom.

ME: Have you ever been in Elgin?
MOM: Why don't you just let a dead dog lie? There's nothing, absolutely nothing wrong with your wonderful family but you. Anyone would go crazy with a father like you. All your women and your crazy ways. Look at that hair!

I've let it grow a little long ever since Brazil. Shelley-Byron-Beethoven.
O.K., let it go, let it drop.
After all the hell I've gone through in the last few years I've become a Buddha, actually (when I started thinking about blowing Christine's brains out with a shotgun when she and Mimi falsely accused me of sexually molesting Chris in order to get total custody) spent more than a year reading Buddhism and Vedanta full-time, doing the breathing and meditation exercises, getting out of myself like a disembodied spirit and peering down at myself and my way of doing things, like I was hanging from the gondola of a hot-air balloon.
And one of the basic things I'd finally faced was that my mother was NUTS! A sado-masochistic freak. And that I'd been trained to have tantrums, that she'd have at me, have

at me, have at me, until I'd finally explode — just in order to survive.

And I'd unconsciously used that *modus operandi* to handle myself in all high-pressure situations, so that every time I was up against the wall being fucked over, I'd blow and blow hard and bad.

"O.K.," I say, unfazed. And not pretending to be unfazed, but genuinely unfazed. Which she can't handle. She can't work her little games on me. She's frustrated out of her fucking mind. "See you later."

"The way you've been with those children, Christopher at the wedding going berserk with those little Chicano brats."

I'm supposed to say "Ecuadorian, not Chicano," at least that. But I don't, just leave, start to look inside myself. Is there a residual anger that I should be worried about? I used to play it cool with her and then erupt into a rage at Christine and the kids within a few days afterwards.

I guess I'm O.K., coming out of and returning into Nothingness, Nirvanaing/extinguishing myself, like crawling into a cave at the bottom of the ocean, like blowing out a match.

What I was supposed to do to Christine and her girlfriend, when they kamakazied in on me and Tanya, was to kill them or at least try. That's what they wanted, I think, to turn me into their executioner. They didn't want each other as much as they wanted death. And that's when I decided to at last perfect/"orientalize" the detachment that had been the ideal presented to me since my childhood. The only difference being that at the center of this Buddhistic mystical experience there wasn't any bright light hidden in a cloud of unknowing/unknowableness, only emptiness, "extinguishment" — which is what Nirvana is all about.

The Buddha's whole point was to stop the entire reincarnation-cycle by blowing himself out like a match. Like hibernating. Deep-freeze. That's what all the Sanskrit words are etymologically related to — the ones that relate to Nirvana. Then Zen turned the blowing-out into a way of life, an epistemology and metaphysics.

Brunch at the Club on Sunday, and Mom starts in on Christopher:

"Another Coke, you're a Cok-e-holic. You get all hyped up and before you know it you need it, you want more and more stimulation, you get into marijuana and then cocaine. You'll be selling your soul for a dose. My husband, your grandfather, used to legally supply morphine addicts with morphine, and I spent many, many hours talking to those poor souls about their addiction. And many times..."

What the hell is she talking about? The kid had a second Coke. He's thirsty.

I get up, take him by the hand.

"Let's go down by the pool."

I feel the rage coming. She hasn't been in this dining room for twenty years. She's got three of her six grandchildren with her at the table. It's a beautiful Michigan June Sunday. The food is great, there really are no problems right now. Within a couple of months, Tanya and I together will be making a hundred thousand a year, Amy will start college in the Fall, Christine is coming up for a visit in another month, the war's over, we're deep into the Heart of Peace.

Hold it down, I say to myself, *hold it down, die a little.*

"Why don't you listen to me? What's wrong with you anyhow, all the education and the lessons we lavished on you!"

Her voice climbs up into shrillness, heads begin to turn, among the heads Polly Holt, the wife of a former university president and an old friend who's heard the whole story about my mother. She winces. I go out the balcony door.

"I'm still hungry," says Chris.

"Let her win," I say to myself, remembering a Tunisian student of mine a few years back telling me — in the midst of the war with Christine — "Lose, that's how you win."

Not that it worked out that way for the Carthaginians.

"I'll get you a hamburger downstairs by the pool," I tell Chris.

The next day Mom leaves; Amy goes back to Kansas.

Mom tries to get me going in the car, at the airport.

"All the education, your father a doctor, and look at you, that belly, that hair! And hanging with Chicanos all the time. What's wrong with Americans? You father's better off dead. All that fat. And now another South American. What's wrong with you?"

On and on and on.

Amy just sat there.

Chris started fooling around with the car radio, found some rock.

"I don't know what's wrong with that boy, he's so hyped-up. All that Coke. No control. All these narcotics. And you were so close to being an M.D."

I tune it out. I'm in the Chinese mystical mountains. I'm a brush painting. The brush. The ink. I'm a Shang dynasty pot. An oracle bone. Zero. Less than zero. Negative numbers lost in deep Zen fog.

That's how I get through it.

Monster Mom leaves first. Then Amy half an hour later.

I hold on tight to Amy for a moment.

"I'm sorry."

"She's really crazy, isn't she?"

Then she's gone and Chris and I play some Double Dragon in the airport arcade. And then it's back home.

Which old witch, the wicked witch.

Silence has never seemed so grand.

Now let's see if we can get back to Christopher full-time.

JUNE 15 — THURSDAY

C hris (according to Christine) isn't supposed to be sleeping in the same bed with Tanya, although Tanya and Christine and the boy all slept in the same bed for his first five years, and he considers Tayna like another mother. That's the way the bonding went. In fact, Christine even always encouraged him to call Tanya Mom too.

I imagine that Christine doesn't want him to sleep with Tanya, because down in Kansas City she feels she can't sleep with him because of Mimi, although I can't see why (at least when they're just sleeping) he just couldn't sleep in the same bed with the two of them.

I was trained to sleep alone, only child and all that. And that's the only way I can sleep. Anyone else in the bed and I freak out, can't sleep. And I keep thinking how sweet it must be to be able to relax in someone's arms with your legs against someone else's legs. I like the idea of Chris sleeping the rest of his life with a woman, liking it, wanting it, needing it.

So the first night I suggested that he sleep in his own bed (as per Christine's orders), but he didn't want to, so he and Tanya and camped out together again. No touching. Separate sides of the bed (I came in and watched them asleep), but still the idea of another presence to go through the night with...

Tanya wants me to have an X-ray of my lungs. I want to wait a while. Don't feel that bad. Only none of my usual remedies are working: high (6 grams/day) doses of Vitamin C, honey, cabbage, garlic, onions. The cough hangs on and a tremendous lassitude hangs over me like a mushroom cloud.

Beginning Monday, Chris has swimming lessons in the mornings, Karate on Thursday evenings. Edita Freeman suggests dance classes. Jonas is taking tap. The East Lansing Arts Workshop has an acting class, but it's filled up. Normally I would have had him signed up two months in advance, but I guess I'm not functioning too normally right now. I feel like I'm trying to hang on to a giant bag of wind, keep it grounded, and it keeps threatening to lift me up and carry me away to Oz and all points *mas allá*.[5]

The pen keeps going all over the page like it has a life of its own.

All Winter and Spring I was writing down lists of things to do when the boy got up here:

1. Make little skit movies like *The Mummy in the Cupboard* (props, two cups of flour and a couple of rolls of gauze), *Swamp Monster Junior* (green face-paint and shoot the whole thing out at North Park), *Dr. Jekyll and Mr. Hyde* (an old Ultima II makeup kit).
2. Start making fantastic kites, kites like giant faces, kites with multiple heads, dragon kites.
3. A week in Chicago with my cousin George and family, see Curt Johnson, Art Institute, Aquarium, etc.
4. Do music quizzes, build up a whole tape-library of "important" works, like Beethoven's 9 symphonies, do music quizzes.

The lists go on. But I don't have the energy to do much of anything. Even this journal. I feel like it's dissolving in my hands.

---

5. *Mas allá* — Spanish for the Great Beyond.

JUNE 16 — FRIDAY
LA BOHÈME & ROBOCOP

Got *La Bohème* this morning from Campus Video. Plus *RoboCop*. Christine on the phone suggested that I bribe him shamelessly. "Whatever works."

So we got through *La Bohème*, except for the silly second act (Musetta in the cafe) which I've never been too impressed by anyhow and which he immediately reacted against. So I skipped to Mimi's death-scene.

I sat reading the titles out for him, crying like a fool.

Could hardly even read them. Like I told the kid, "Every time I see Mimi and Rudolpho, I keep thinking of me and your mother."

And not just on the surface either. Every time I talk to her on the phone she comes up with another profile of her own problems. Something wrong with her heart, her immune system. She sounds like death warmed over every night when I talk to her/let her talk to the kid. And now I'm on the way down too.

"Go and get the X-ray, do what Tanya says," she said tonight.

I don't want to know. I'd rather not know. Or maybe I already know the whole story.

Videotaped *La Bohème*, and tonight, after Tanya got home from the hospital, watched *RoboCop*.

Goddamned kit wanted to re-see every head getting splattered all over the landscape. He's a gruesome ghoul. When he was four and five all he wanted to see was horror films, but they scared him so much that he'd wake up screaming every night.

I've never seen anyone with such a vivid imagination. Not even myself. I can push the Imagination Button and away I go, but with him Imagination takes over. That's all there is! He can't seem to release it, to un-push the button.

Videotaped him after the viewing, asked him questions about the film. Trying to get him to think, think about film, think about anything, and learn how to talk, get an easy flow between Head and Tongue.

He said some interesting things, like "I liked RoboCop himself, how he was made. And doing the whole thing on location. Very realistic."

I talked a little about the old Buck Rogers films, *The Shape of Things to Come, Metropolis.*

"We're going to have to get a video-disk player, build up a whole film history library."

"Great!"

Little by little.

Anything, any field, any subject, can "work" for people if you let it.

The importance of verisimilitude. Why audiences actually applaud the sets in *La Bohème* when they're really convincing. It's gotta flow the way life flows. Which is why I like Eric Rohmer's films so much — *Full Moon Over Paris, A Night at Maud's, Claire's Knee.*

Got a little bit into "pacing" and "plot structure."

I liked the flashbacks into Officer Murphy's pre-RoboCop past. Picture of Old Detroit frightening, but not too far from fact. Acting top notch.

Before he came up I taped a whole box of tapes for the kid. Played some Bruckner tonight before he went to bed, Tanya read him some *Pico Pau Amarelo* in Portuguese. Would like to take him to Brazil next summer (their winter) if I'm still around. You can't get inside another country's skin until you get inside the language, and until you get inside another country's skin, you're condemned to the worst kind of chauvinistic isolation. You can't time-travel, can't really get into Neanderthal skin and pray to the great elephant god Toro-Teo, the returning solstice sun.[6]

JUNE 17 — SATURDAY
JEDERMANN

T anya off. Over to North Park, took a long walk out into the forest. Very lush, wet year. I've got to always watch out for poison ivy, don't want to spend another summer all bandaged up.

Brought my *Siegfried* tape with me, cassette player on an old leather shoelace around my neck.

"You're a fanatic, aren't you!" said Tanya as we walked through swamp and forest and Siegfried was forging his sword, Wotan appearing, then Siegfried fighting Fafner.

I don't know why it doesn't capture the boy's imagination more. I ought to re-write it as a novel, do it as a cartoon, make it more accessible. It's a great, for the most part unappreciated, masterpiece. Although sometimes I think I'd rather just hear it than see it, let Fafner become the size of a mountain in my mind. Like old radio — *The Shadow, I Love a Mystery.*

But Chris (the audio-visual mind) never seems to go for heroes like *Masters of the Universe.* He loved *RoboCop,* loved (past tense) *The Return of the Living Dead* and had a long-time flirtation with Michael Jackson's *Thriller.*

---

6. A reference to a 300,000 B.C. find in Spain, elephant bones arranged to point toward the sunrise on the day of the Winter Solstice. Brian claimed the bones formed a proto-letter T.

I could really see him going into making horror films. All he really lacks is patience. He can't focus! They're right about that much in Kansas City. But TIME... how much could I focus at 8?!

I finally had to stop in the middle of our hike. Cool day, but I broke out into a sweat, like when you break a leg, that kind of debilitating, black-out sweat.

Tanya wanted me to go down to Sparrow emergency tonight, but I refused. I'm like Lynne Savitt, who told me that if she were diagnosed with breast cancer, she'd refuse any treatment whatsoever: "I'm going out of life with the same equipment I came in with."

What I myself feel is a kind of total, what's the word, cynicism/fatalism regarding Medicine. When you're going to go, one thing I learned, having a doctor for a father, having gone to Med School, being married to a doctor, is the helplessness/uselessness of Medicine when the final axe-blow comes down.

What I mainly hate about being sick is how it distances me from my world, from what I believe in. And even from the boy himself.

I find hatred that I thought I'd left behind in India (with the Buddha) welling up inside me again. Nastiness showing itself, like under the Buddha mask what I really am is a bulging-eyed Japanese temple demon.

That's the way I was through my whole first marriage. That's what I was raised to be: a Little Lord Fountleroy Monster. On the one hand, coddled and spoiled; on the other, regimented into a kind of full-time childhood-music concentration camp, the beat of the metronome, the rhythm of the goosestep grand opera.

Today Chris wanted to stop at Arby's to get some Ghost Busters plastic cup. Something he saw advertised on

TV. A simple thing. I've got the money — and time. My plan was to take off the whole summer and (except for 3 hours a week in class) devote myself entirely to the boy. This is supposed to be Paradise Garden, the Great Good Place.

So he said he wanted to stop at Arby's and I swerved into Arby's parking lot, almost knocked him out of his seat, fuck the guy behind me, almost wishing that some cop would have seen me and pulled me back into reality with a ticket.

Got him his plastic cup, bitched him out.

"Is there anything else the Little Lord wants? Maybe to get sent back to Kansas City?!"

The cancer talking, not me.

Waiting three years to get him up here, and then slashing at him like that. What's the point? And what's the point, really, of all the lofty Gothic structures of art, music, literature — if I have no charity. And I don't have it. God knows, at least for a moment I didn't have it.

One afterthought — my mother's visit this time is like one of those sci-fi films of possession by the Thing. She's the Thing inside me and I'm not really me. And then slowly the line between the me and the Thing gets blurred and It takes over.

Is this whole art/literature thing called Civilization really Civilization, or is it — in my case, anyhow — some sort of little Nazi regime that was imposed on me by my parents because it was a symbolic ladder up which I was supposed to climb out of the middle- to the upper-class? My Bohemian girl-secretary mother's passport to respectability. Something to show off when I'd go over to my cousins' houses at Christmas or Thanksgiving and pound out a few minuets for them on their eternally untuned pianos?

And I know how I feel physically. It's the last act of Everyman — I'm being surrounded. Like the way they used to do it in medieval (Catholic) Germany, "Jedermann!"

screamed out from the four corners of a square, "Jedermann!" And I hate it. I hate the boy for all the years he'll
have without me. I hate Tanya for her next husband. I hate
them all for the slow forgetfulness that will overtake them as
I become more and more erased. A little bit of history, then
a little bit of legend, then totally replaced by the living.

Like how much do I really think about my father or even
my grandmother — really? Not how much I feel I should
remember them as some sort of homage to the dead, but
how much, in the normal flow and flux of my thoughts, they
really come in and haunt me.

They're gone, I'll be gone. And I wouldn't be surprised
if — in twenty years — Christine and Tanya end up with a
house on Tanya's property on Santa Catarina off the southern
Brazilian coast, two old ladies, a yearly visit from Christopher
Well, I'll haunt them, the sons of bitches, I'll circle through
their dreams like a giant, white vampire bat.

I hardly sleep any more. At the same time am always
tired. I keep thinking about all those Adrenalin-like com-
pounds secreted by malignant tumors. What's happening to
my mind? The Great Good Place is slowly becoming The
Minor Hell-Hole, and I'm back to where I never left — my
Aunt Daisy, Kokoschka, Egon Schiele, Artaud.

JUNE 18 — SUNDAY
THE VERDICT

Tried to get up for church — 11:30. Wanted to go over to
brunch. But I felt like I was underwater. Memories of gall-
bladders and fractured arms and polio. There comes a time
when you give up, you're not making it, give yourself up to
the medics and take your chances, no matter how slim.

Down to Sparrow Emergency for an X-ray. It took about two hours, Chris fucking around the whole time, almost running into accident cases, almost knocking down plastic-hipped old ladies on crutches. Anger/loathing/violence unwinding inside me like the Mother of All Anacondas.

Doctor on call motioning to Tanya to come into his office with him.

Big secret.

And she, the perfect conspirator, comes back in to where I'm waiting, a little graver than even her usual tomb-stone gravity. "Grave" — the right word for her all around.

"Well, what's the big medical verdict?"

No answer. No reaction.

"It wouldn't kill you to show some emotion, for crissake, what am I, a train you just get off?"

She turns, leaves me alone, the nurse comes in with a sign-out sheet for me to sign. That's it. We're in the car going home.

"You want to tell me, or is it some big mortician's convention secret?"

"There's a massive tumor in your left lung, you'll need a biopsy first, but..."

Pause for Brazilian soap-opera (novella) effect.

"And?"

"It's premature to say, but I'd guess it's spread to the liver..."

"Which gives me how much time?"

"There's no timetable. With chemotherapy and radia-tion..."

"Come on!"

"A couple... a few months."

I glance back at Chris in the back seat. He looks so much like his mother, like a very, very little kid again, a fragile

Dalton China doll, a Beatrix Potterish dormouse caught in a fragile frozen moment of unguarded surprise.

JUNE 19 — MONDAY
I'LL HAVE ALL ETERNITY TO REST

When I talked to Christine this morning, she said: "Have Tanya bring the boy back immediately by plane. Why let him see you this way, what's the point?"

"Let's imagine I'd waited another month before I got the verdict."

"But could you have waited?"

"Well, no one's bringing him back," I say in cloudy, floating defiance. Debussy's *Nuages* again.[7] Thinking of Debussy writing his fake Greek, artsy-fartsy "Songs of Bilitis" when he was dying of bowel cancer, had already had a colostomy.

"I'll try to get up there in a week," she says, "let me talk to Tanya."

Tanya gets on the phone — upstairs.

I don't even try to listen in downstairs. Let them dance their little Danse Macabre together.

*****

NOTE. *There is a break here in the original manuscript. The diary was written in a perfect-bound unlined notebook. A couple of pages were torn out. Whether Brian himself tore them out or someone else did a little censoring is anybody's guess. H.F.*

*****

---

7. *Nuages* — Clouds. One of Debussy's orchestral nocturnes.

the difference, I'm wiped out almost full-time anyhow. Even this pen on this paper is an agony. It's like rain falling inside me, as if I'm slowly, very slowly, scuba-diving to the bottom of the sea or rising up in a helium balloon — up, up, up into the unbreathable stratosphere. The two unbreatheable poles of my private hell.

I sit by the edge of the pool and watch the boy learning how to swim. The only father (the only male) except for the swimming coach. Also no Blacks, no Chicanos, although there are two Chinese-White kids.

It's as if the 50's and 60's and 70's never happened, the sexual revolution, the racial revolution. Business as usual.

And then you start watching the all-white middle class women among themselves and you start to see a whole subtle Queen of the Mountain moral wrestling matching taking place. It's the pecking order. And there's a particular kind of willowy, very white, very anemic, snobby-looking type that always seems to end up at the top of the pecking order. But the top dog (top bird) perch is so precarious, everyone else is always looking for a chance to topple her.

This afternoon we went over to Tebida's house. Her $165,000.00 (I asked) house. And the father's only, what, an Associate Professor in the School of Veterinary Medicine, wife not working at all. Can't be a lot of money circulating around.

We sat by the pool, the father, mother and I, Tebida and his two sisters in the water with Chris.

A beautiful interlude. For a moment I wasn't sick at all.

They talked about Uganda in the old days, the sanity of family structures versus the dissolving structures here. I could just as well have been talking to Bolivians or Tunisians or Malaysians. Color is such an irrelevancy. I told them about my last trip to Bolivia to Mariano Baptista's, how I never wanted to leave.

Malaysians. Color is such an irrelevancy. I told them about
my last trip to Bolivia to Mariano Baptista's, how I never
wanted to leave.

"The house, my old friend from the old days in Caracas,
the tile ceiling in the kitchen, the red tile floors, the whole
sense of the colonial that surrounds you in La Paz. You're
back a couple hundred years anyhow. And Mariano's wife,
Carmen, had her mother living with her, this old German
who reminded me of my Czech grandmother. The old lady
would take me into the kitchen at night and give me something to eat, and talk, talk, talk about the past, cry, tell me
about her husband's murder — Bolivian politics. I loved the
opening up. I used to be so content with just *being* when I
was a kid. With Chris it's a whole other game — he can't sit
still."

"None of them can nowadays," said John, Tebida's father.
"What worries me is what they're going to do when they
grow up. If they can't sit still, can't apply themselves to
anything, what are they going to do in life?"

"They can always be film- and TV-critics, I suppose," I
smiled.

I told them about my cancer.

"But shouldn't you be...?" Francis started to say.

Be what? Be!

"It doesn't make any difference. I have my radiation
session later this afternoon. The rest of the time..."

"But shouldn't you be resting?" insisted Francis.

"I'll have all eternity to rest," I answered dramatically.

But I wasn't kidding. All this chemotherapy-radiation crap
is a good way for the hospital to cash in on my insurance, but
medically it's all a free-fall down, a countdown before I hit the
ground.

I seemed to have dozed off and they let me sleep, woke up a little sunburned, got to my radiation therapy late.

Tonight Chris chose the film over at Meijers. *Interface*. I filmed part of the film, then him watching it. Slow film. The lowest of budgets. Must have been all shot in some junior college in Southern California. A bunch of computer students find this hidden chamber in the basement of the college (number-one implausibility), put on these masks with voice-altering microphones in them (why?), and start to play vigilante.

"Too slow," said Chris.

I talked a little about shit actors — which they all were — and inherent plot-implausibilities that block any real suspension of belief. Once you believe Middle Kingdoms or Hobbits exist, O.K., but before then... of course, C.S. Lewis, Tolkien, that whole Oxford bunch, were such Norse scholars, it all has this ancient mythological base to it. *Interface* is all surface-improvisation.

Then upstairs. Bathe.

It's such a shitty way to die. It bothered Chris that I've gotten so fucking *thin*.

"It really goes fast, doesn't it," I said to Tanya. She looked sad, confused. The confusion's a new twist. Of course, she hasn't had that much experience with lung cancer. Mainly reconstructive (facial) surgery. I used to kid her about it: "Glorified seamstress." And the irony is that she always wanted to go into dress-designing.

Then read to Chris. I lay down on the bed looking through the doorway that separates his bedroom from hers. The walls of his room are filled with racks with bugs in them, plus posters of Beethoven (and RoboCop); on his closet door hang all the programs of plays I've taken him to over the years:

BARNUM
THE SOUND OF MUSIC
THE TEMPEST
THREE-PENNY OPERA
MIDSUMMER NIGHT'S DREAM
CAMINO REAL
AH, WILDERNESS...

Just tons of stuff. Even when he was four or five I'd take him to see a Shakespeare play, especially if it was fun like *A Midsummer Night's Dream.* Give him the idea beforehand, read a few key scenes, even draw some pictures, like Bottom with a donkey's head on, or I'd ask him "What do you think a wicked, lazy earth spirit (Caliban) would/should look like," and he'd give it a try. The same with Ariel, the "air spirit." Then we'd go see how they really looked on stage.

And if he didn't want to stay for the whole play, I'd never force him. Like the free plays down at LCC in the summer. We'd see one act one night, another act another night, bits and pieces here and there. And then sometimes (*Of Mice and Men,* for example) he'd want to see the whole thing all over again from the beginning to the end.

I don't know how much is sticking, can stick, will stick. I think, in deep-down, dark, hidden levels, a lot! I still remember the first time I saw *Carmen* like it was yesterday.

Tomorrow I'm going to try Bergman's version of *The Magic Flute.* When I was twelve I played Sarastro. My voice had just changed.

The Religion of Humanism.

Not much else in this post-Gothic, post-Vatican II, Post-Reformed Movement media-trivia world to carry us into the heart of the Great Mystery. Maybe Wagner's leading us into the center of Teutonic myth (I'm thinking of when, after Siegfried kills Fafner and tastes the dragon-blood, he learns how to understand the "speech" of birds) is the closest we can get nowadays to revelation.

Paris, I was 20, every morning into the stone forest (thinking of Ruskin's remarks on Gothic cathedrals as reproductions of forests) of Notre Dame Cathedral, feeling the Mystery of the Incarnation, as if it had really happened. But since then?

Under the culture-vulture Buddha masks, still the little boy looking for/into/through Mystery.

TUESDAY — JUNE 20
I COULDN'T WALK THAT FAR

It looks like Christine's coming up to take the boy back in about another week. In a way, maybe it's better after all. Too much pain, a sense of falling, failing.,

Blew up at the boy again today. Out walking the two dogs. He wanted to go to a park five or six blocks away where I used to always take him when he was younger. I remember one Fall, the sky clouding over with snow-clouds, my saying "Here comes the Snow Queen, you can see her robes," and he'd gotten all afraid. What an imagination! Like the horror films he always wants to watch, *Friday the 13th, Nightmare on Elm Street* (the whole series), and then they take over his dreams. Like that *Nightmare on Elm Street* film itself, *The Dream-Master.*

Only I couldn't walk six blocks today.

"Jesus, can't you understand, I can't do it, I'm dying from cancer!" As loud as I could scream. Which isn't too loud these days. "Your mother will be up here in another week, and then the agony ends, at least as far as you're concerned.

You can go down to Kansas City and walk as much as you want, and I can die in peace."

He started to cry.

Like *Die Götterdämmerung*, it all falls down and goes boom on a massive, cosmic scale. But I really couldn't walk that far, didn't want to try and then not be able to make it, ending up sitting on someone's lawn unable to move.

Went down to Impression Five museum this afternoon after struggling through my stupid summer-school class and before my radiation treatment.

He refused to look at a balance and learn what torque is:

$$TORQUE = WEIGHT \times DISTANCE.$$

Just wouldn't stop for one minute, like he's sprayed with knowledge-repellent or something. I almost blew up again.

Talked about it with Tanya in the kitchen while she was warming up a TV dinner for him.

"You're undoing everything you've done," she said, "I think Christine's right, just let him go."

"How about my going? Down to Tiawanaku, Atacama, the sacred places, in time for the Winter solstice, watch the Old Sun die and be replaced by the Morning Star New Sun. Get the fuck out of here," I said bitterly. She's such a, I don't know, LIZARD.

Totally ignored me (lizardishly), of course. Cynic, stoic, fatalist. I'm her property now — dying property, but still property. And then she pulled an about-face and insisted on cutting my hair tonight, like I was a kid.

The amazing thing about Christopher is his, what can I call it, steadfastness/faithfulness. He's neither afraid of me (even at my worst) nor does he ever, really, think about cutting with me — this indestructible blood-bonding. Like he always used to tell his mother when he'd get in trouble in school and try to blame it on me: "I'm just like my Daddy, we're like twins."

THE MAGIC FLUTE

Tonight went well. I loved the "innocence" of the whole presentation. That'd be a good title for a book about Mozart: *The Innocence of Mozart.* Not a touch of anything prurient about the man. And the same goes for Bergman: *The Innocence of Ingmar Bergman.*

And the presentation was pure 18th century, with those Bergman moments of interiorized, mystical quietude.

Chris liked the magic bells, the magic flute, the dragon. But what he really likes is a bullet of a production like *RoboCop* — violence, quick, dovetailed, non-stop violence.

Then a bath, reading time. I come in ("Just two minutes.") with Rilke's *Sonnets to Orpheus.* Just a little German for the boy:

> *Dass doch einer, ein Schauender, endlich ihren*
> *   langen Bestand*
> *staunend begriffe und rühmte. Nur dem*
> *   Aufsingenden*
> *säglich.*
> *Nur dem Göttlichen hörbar.*

I read the German first, then tried to translate it.

> If only anyone, a See-er, finally understood
>   and praised its worth.
> Only sung by the singer.
> Only heard by the god.

"It seems to be a sonnet about gold, but it really isn't. It's about catching *being* between the cracks — epiphanal, hierophantic moments, God-seeing, God-revealing moments. It's about a *Schauender*. Like the English *show*. Like a *show-er*. A *see-er*. Only the singer can say it. Only a god can hear it. Like those quiet moments in *The Magic Flute*."

Tanya and Chris looking at each other. Blank.

"What Rilke always is talking about is the intensification of the perception of the Now."

Still pretending zero, but they know what I mean. You don't have to drape yourself with stars out in the Atacama Desert in order to understand mystery.

"O.K.," I said, "well, I love you both, see you in the morning."

Not that there aren't vast distances between us. The 1990's (them) versus shamanistic pre-history (me).

Kisses all around. But hollow. Feeling it all run down, the illusion of permanence, and then the reality of illusion.

Wir haben nur einmal, einmal gewesen zu sein...
We only have once, once to be...

Rilke would just sit around and wait for the terrible angels inside him to appear. *Schreckliche Englen*.

I eat a mango, spray on a little OFF, out to the front porch listening to a Schoenberg orchestration of a Brahms Quartet for Piano and Strings (Opus 25), Paul Carter, the mad musico from next door coming home, sees me.

"I hear you're sick," he says. "You look fine."

"Just an intermediate phase," I say.

"Well, I hope you feel better," he says.

Long hair and boots. Claims he's a pagan/primitivist. Candles and ouija boards. "The Christian Devil is the pre-Christian God," he told me one day. Trying to hang onto something. Try the stars! But he's a good guy anyhow.

Then the phone ringing. I came inside, pulled off my earphones.

Horse Morse from San Francisco. Wrote him last week.

"What's all this shit about lung cancer? How bad is it?"

"It's confirmed. Maybe I've got two months, maybe one fully conscious one. Although even now it's a little 'foggy bottom' for me."

"You want me to come out?"

"Tanya wouldn't appreciate it, and Christine's coming next week to take the kid back. Although I'd love to see you."

"What's she taking him back for? I'd think it'd be exactly the opposite — especially leave him there now. Be there herself."

"Don't ask me. I don't know. I don't change toward people, I really don't. And you're right, let the boy see death. Get the picture."

"You want me to call her?"

"Call her, and she'll be here tomorrow. Maybe I should come out there and die facing Saucelito."

"Not so crazy. You're welcome," he says with no hesitation, "What the fuck am I supposed to do for old friends? Last year it was Todd Lawson, now you."

"That's what happens to the survivors. I remember asking my mother's 93-year-old boyfriend a few years ago, 'What's the worst thing about surviving to 93?' His answer: 'The loneliness.'"

"I'm sorry," he says weakly, always awkward on the phone, but this is too much.

"I would like to see you."

"Maybe after the kid's gone."

"O.K."

"Take it easy."

"Thanks for the call."

Maybe after the kid's gone; maybe (more likely) not at all.

I go through the bottom for a long moment, just sit there at the dining room table. What, 25 years I've known him. My father confessor. 25 years of weekly letters.

I go upstairs to my room, lie down, worn out, but I don't want to give into it. It's as if the life in me is hungrier than ever for every last possible conscious moment.

A little more Rilke before I sleep.

Die junge Nacht

The young night

liegt wie ein köhler Duft

lies like a cool breeze

auf dem Canal

on the canal

Der Fremde steht und trinkt

the stranger stays and drinks

den Klang

every note

verloren im seine Seele

lost in his soul

vorrei morir
— I want to die.....

It's a game he's playing. When you really have to die all
you can think about is life.

WEDNESDAY, JUNE 21

Sitting at the pool this morning. They're painting the
WKAR transmission towers so the FM was off, switched
over to the AM station. Rebroadcast of BBC News. Funny
listening to the BBC. Like the old days in Spain the year
Franco died, and you had to listen to BBC in Valencia to find
out what was happening in Madrid.

All the news that seems totally outside the U.S. orbit.
Trouble in Kabul, the Tamil Tigers stirring up trouble again.
I suppose there's 10 other people in town besides myself
who even know what Tamil IS. I used to get all these letters
from the Tamil Society in India because I'd written two
paragraphs in one of my books, very theoretically comparing
Tamil to Maya.

Along came Bernice Bishop, sat down next to me.
Retired now, she tells me she's 68. Flesh melting a little on
her bones, but she looks good. Has this whole story about
her boy-friend's wife finding out about her and her husband,
coming over to her place the night before and screaming into
the downstairs microphone of the intercom system.

I told her: "You ought to rejoice that you're still capable of such carryings-on at 68!"

She complimented me on my weight-loss. I'm getting a little tan. It hides reality. Why say anything else? I didn't. What should I do, go around wearing a death's head on my T-shirt?

Then class at noon. If I don't write about class, it's because I don't think about class. I've never seen such a bunch of fuck-offs in my life before. Trying to do a class on literary criticism — how to write it. Subject matter — U.S. poets in the last 30 years. My "club" — Bukowski, the two Bennetts, Winans, Richard Morris, Beining, Luschei. Like a course in the Poets of Atlantis, the Poets of the Gobi Desert, the Poets of the Valley of Kings.

The attendance isn't sporadic, but insulting. One very intense guy, tall, stiff, dark-skinned, Latino-looking, reminds me of the young Rudolph Hess, and there's an intense English major with lots of hair who wants to write a paper on my poetry. Tickle my ego a little. I can use it.

But most of them are indifferent to the fact that Rilke is dying right there in front of them. We always see the poets and painters through the lens of an appreciative after-the-fact critical evaluation, but never the artists themselves as seen (without their post-mortem numinosity about them) by their contemporaries.

Then dragged myself back to Impression Five this afternoon, a demo on how to make "Slime" — polyvinyl alcohol and borax + vinyl. The paint forms another polymer with the borax-alcohol polymer.

Then Chris got into trouble in the "touch tunnel." He and some other kids were standing in the entrance scaring the kids as they came in. I look at him and all I see is kinetic energy. Like lightning or the sea, neither good nor evil, it just

IS. The only problem being that it remains totally unharnessed. I don't know, I can't imagine him with a job, married, a father. I think of him as the Eternal Kid. Of course, that's true for all of us. How could I ever imagine Baby Babs as the monster she is now?!

He seems to have no sense of my gradual descent into hell, after the museum wanted to walk along the riverfront. So I did. Maybe it's good for me. Saw a set down by the "sun-bowl," actors rehearsing.

A dramatization of *The Odyssey*, high-school students in a special summer program at Lansing Community College.

"I want to come tonight," he says.

Which cheered me up immensely.

This slow straightening-out of the spirit, our own private de Chardinian Omega Points, not necessarily to touch the Cosmic Christ, but the Cosmic Purpose in all of us straining toward (I'm thinking of Shaw's, not Nietzsche's *Man and Superman*) the next step in evolution — Homo aestheticus. Our whole body/life just a support-system for religious-aesthetic experiences.

My father should have taken his own advice and instead of sticking me into music, should have kept going at it himself.

Just to *imagine* him as violinist, maybe not even as a soloist, but with the Chicago Symphony stuck someplace in the second violins. Instead of all that lugubrious, unhappy M.D. bullshit.

Image that comes to mind. When I was studying for my role as Sarastro in *The Magic Flute*, Mrs. Metzger had me go and study with Andy Foldi. I was 12, he must have been in his twenties.

Down in Inglewood. South Side of Chicago, the satellite ring area around the University of Chicago. Old greystone building. I remember the creaky wooden floors, the wooden doors between rooms that slid into the walls, the old piano, bookcases filled with the kinds of books we never bought — portfolio-sized books on Michelangelo, Raphael, the Impressionists, Greek sculpture.

My problem was pitch, so he'd go into "pitch-context," the half- and whole-tones surrounding a particular note.

And what I felt in his presence was a kind of religious awe, like I was in an old Amsterdam synagogue, Rembrandt on the search for one of those magnificent, old Jewish holy faces. Art had become not a substitute for religion, but its extension/incarnation, the way it always had been, of course, whether at Altamira or Delphi or Tiawanaku or Chartres... which makes the Impressionists the high-priests of what existential/being-and-nothingness God?

Really *floating* right now, throw an anchor down...

Went to *The Odyssey* tonight. They followed the original structure very tightly, the appearances of the gods and goddesses, without which the whole narrative machinery becomes very iffy.

Circe, the Cyclops, Aeolus.

Afterwards Chris waxed eloquent. Right on target.

"I really liked it, the story. I just had a hard time believing in the characters. They all seemed so young."

They were. Young...and the girls startlingly beautiful.

Went over to Castellani's afterwards for some canolli, capuchin, and (for Chris) root beer.

"I like it here," he says.

It's an old Italian grocery-store atmosphere with marble-topped tables. Castelanni's grandfather had had the original store down in Lansing, then his father, now him. Imported groceries and wines, the canolli made right there. But it's iffy whether he's going to survive or not. Students like the chrome-hubcap, inauthentic places. Instant atmosphere instead of the real thing. Cafe Venezia, where the only thing

Venetian about it is a big photo of St. Mark's Plaza, next to the espresso machine.

I kept drifting back to Old Chicago again. Dolores Volini and the Near North Side, the portrait of her grandfather on the wall of the downstairs library. 1611 N. Dearborn Parkway, just next to the beginning of Lincoln Park, the area that spelled out Old Money in big brass address numbers.

My first real encounter with Patrician Epicureanism (as in Pater's *Marius the Epicurean*). Funny the things that rattle around in your memory like walnuts loose in their shells.

I remember Dolores' sister, Marcella, getting ready for her wedding and talking about having a string quartet up in the organ loft, talking about what they were going to play, a little Bach, a little Gabrieli, a little Fauré, a little Frescobaldi, I forget...

Jim Keller was working at Castellani's. Has just finished law school.

I wanted to hook him for Amy when she was up for the winter last winter. Not just because his grandfather and father are millionaire lawyers (although a little kick-start inheritance doesn't hurt), but because of the whole sense of stability, tradition, continuity he radiates.

There's this immense downgrading of the American Dream, so many people with these spider-web lives, and all that still sustains us is the continuity of the Aristoi, Lampedusa's *Leopardo*.

What I'd like for all my kids is an unbroken sense of, let's call it "on-trackness," stretching through their lives.

What I felt in Bolivia, I suppose, at Mariano and Carmen's, not sad time stretching before and after, but tranquil time, secure time, time that knows what it is and where it's going. My mind full of images of leather-sofaed libraries and quiet, thick-walled brownstones on tree-lined streets, the three bears, the ten bears (Dolores has 9 brothers and sisters), early morning (light) Mass/its equivalents...

Keller asked about Amy and I told him she was down in Kansas City again — this time trying to sell vacuum cleaners. "You look emaciated," he said.

"I'm fasting," I answered, "to lose a little weight." Why tell him? Why not just quietly drop off the edge of the world and disappear?

He hadn't wanted Amy because she wasn't Jewish.

"I'd blow my family away if I married a Goy."

"Well, we can always solve that," I'd answered him. All the times I'd talked to Menke about my converting to Judaism, something I can really believe in, instead of the desupernaturalized wet toast that Post-Vatican II Catholicism has become. Just a couple of weeks ago, Father What's-His-Name explaining the miracle of the loaves and fishes by saying that "everyone travelling through the desert has hidden food, what Jesus did was to activate generosity," or, when confronted with "What God has joined together, let no man put asunder," to say "facing so many divorced couples in the congregation, I'm embarrassed by today's Gospel!" Embarrassed by the Gospel?!

Katz even told me that "I have the power to make you a Jew, I have a rabbinical degree from Yeshiva."

But Keller still backed down, said he wasn't really ready to settle down. Not that Amy, at 17, is ready to settle down either, but what's wrong with a long engagement. I'm not talking about settling down anyhow — maybe about un-settling a little bit, shaking things up. *I come not to bring peace but the sword.* Tired of fatalistic, comfortable mediocrity.

Then home to bed. A little bit of Wagner for Chris. Siegfried wakes Brunhilde, that initial love-duet when the two of them merge heroically into one.

I wonder if I should even keep this diary going.

It's one a.m., fan blowing on me. I feel like I'm adrift in deep space.

The radiation technician at Sparrow's a woman about my age. The whole time she's working with me she's on the edge of tears. You'd think that after 25 years of working mostly with the dying, that she'd get used to it. Or maybe I'm an especially personal case for her. The way I unintentionally, instinctively (my old Czech grandmother) turn everything into an instantaneous little village. Like we've known each other for a thousand years.

THURSDAY — JUNE 22

Took Chris out by the farms tonight to see the evening sky, Venus just above the horizon, a little below and to the left of Pollux and Castor, the twins...

Then talked to him a little about ancient myth.

"That's all anyone lived for. Like the story of Ishtar going through seven gates into the Underworld, at every gate taking off some jewels, being followed into the Underworld by this boatman in his boat. It's really Venus in the Fall, the receding from the Earth (the taking off of the jewels), then Mars (the boatman) inside a crescent moon (the boat) following Venus over the horizon. That's the Babylonian legend. Among the Greeks it's Orpheus with his lyre/harp, Mars (Orpheus) inside the crescent moon, which is the lyre, following Venus (Eurydice) down into the Underworld — which simply means over the horizon."

"Can I go to Seven-Eleven for a slurpie now?" he asks.

"Why not?"

And that's where we go. Then — at his insistence — to Pinball Pete's to play a little Splatter House, this gruesome character with a hockey mask on (like Jason in the *Friday the Thirteenth* films), going through basements and axing all these corpses and bloodsuckers. Only that's too hard for him. So he moves over to Superman, which is a little bit easier, Double Dragon, which gives him the most for his quarter.

All I can give him are a couple dollars a day.

Three years ago, when his mother hit me with a car, I got double insurance to the tune of $8,000 (multiple fractured right arm, just fragments, really, held together by metal plates and screws), but now I'm down to my last $75.00. Trips to the Atacama Desert with Twyla, TV's, clothes, trips to New York, little presents all the time, a continuous procession of gifts from me to my kids, their mother, their mother's sister.

Why not? And now we're down to the end in all ways.

"Why don't I get a leave of absence, borrow some money to live on. Just stay home full-time. You can't really do it alone," Tanya said today.

"But I'm doing it," I answered.

Dragging myself out of bed in the morning, dragging myself over to the pool, dragging myself to class, dragging myself to the video store, dragging myself to Pinball Pete's, dragging, dragging, dragging, running down, non-rechargeable batteries, mornings like midnights, midnights like Judgement Day, three-quarters gone, one quarter to go.

Don't really want her around full-time. She already radiates enough deep melancholy/fatalism. Let her go to work. There's always the last act in the hospital. Until then...

Why do I see her like a vulture descending from the heavens beginning its feast on dead water-buffalo-me with the anus — the easiest place to begin with?

"Why not let up a little," she insisted. "Why push it?"

"Let me push it as long as I can. It hardly makes any difference."

"You're wasting your time."

"Not for long!"

A few more weeks. What? And then the boy has seventy years without me. Don't tell me I'm wasting my time, that all we are is leaves and snow. What's that poem by Hopkins, immortal diamond. *We are what Christ was, immortal diamond!* All of Hopkins' thrust toward creating an aesthetics where our "thisness" somehow counts, so we aren't just *les nieges d'hier* (last year's snows), melting, evaporating. A site like Nazca or La Venta. Who lived there? What were their names? What did they believe? How can you believe in immortality when you open a tomb and see five-thousand-year-old bones?

Watched an old Captain American film this afternoon.

Like the Paleolithic Age of Sci-Fi films, the fifty-cent shield, the low-budget, doctored-up motorcycle. And the plot's always the same, some madman-criminal gets a poison or a bomb of some kind and blackmails the national government for a million dollars.

Acting primitive, sets primitive, plot primitive — even Chris recognized that.

"It's kind of hard to believe in, isn't it?"

Verisimilitude.

Thinking at the pool this morning the whole time about sociological determinism and the two ways of life — Continuity versus Fragmentation.

The Jews always in the back of my mind. Such a small "tribe" of people, but such an impact on the world. If you just think about it, THE BIBLE, Christ, TALMUD, Spinoza, KABALLAH, Marx, Mahler, Einstein, Salk, Gershwin... this endless list. Because there's always the sense of the Chosen People, family, ethics, Hebrew School, continuity. What is TALMUD, after all, but an endless discussion about how to deal with the vagaries of life?

Then you smash the family, take out continuity, ethics, education, the sense of purpose, change Chosen to Cursed, and what do you have?   Detroit.

Looking at the boy in the pool thinking about all the shit he's been through in the last few years, facing the fact that Christine has deep emotional problems, walking out on her teaching job five years ago, getting fired, never since then really getting back on any track, a couple of science-courses, but then stopping taking courses altogether, just waiting for Mimi to get a grant of some kind to set up a lab so that then she can work with her. And if the grant never comes, I guess she'll never work. No insurance, empty days, Mimi finishing medical school. But what is Christine finishing? Always the same overwhelming sense of purposelessness in her life, her father like a giant negative force (black umbrella) overshadowing her entire life. Magnet and iron-filings. As if she doesn't have a will of her own.

NORM
NORMALITY
UNITY
CONTINUITY

versus

FREAKISHNESS
ABNORMALITY
DISUNITY
DISCONTINUITY

The City of Dis *versus* the City of Light (God).

She'd even tried the same dependency game with me, but I was always pushing her to write criticism, get on the tenure track in the department, create her own image/purpose/destiny. Now she's back on the coattails of someone else's destiny again.

The boy actually swimming now. Ready to jump off the big board.

How much have I already passed on? How much good, how much evil? To have even thought that Christine and I could have just brought Tanya into the marriage and it would have all worked out...

Talk about *her* profound mental problems, what about *mine*?

FRIDAY — JUNE 23
MUSIC IN MY HEAD

Took Chris to see *Who's Afraid of Virginia Woolf?* Tonight. A play about sick games.

Then I came home and was reading about the courtship behavior of Kittiwakes in Tinbergen's *Curious Naturalists*, how Kittiwake courtship is a combination of love and hate, sex and aggression, always on the edge of warfare. And I got to thinking about me and Christine, how maybe what we had was the perfect tension (between love and aggression) needed to produce kids, and now, three kids later, that whole phase is over, she doesn't need a male, she can return to the female world of her childhood, her father ensconced in the living room, her mother, two sisters, Great Aunt Mabel and Grandmother all in the kitchen drinking coffee and chomping on cookies. The exclusively female-centered kitchen, a bi-polar world of male-female territoriality. Is that what's under the Lesbian cover? Or did bringing Tanya into the marriage destroy all the dynamics of interaction between the two of us? Maybe monogamy is instinctive. Solomon and his thousand wives — and all the problems the harem brought with it.

There's all these hidden behavior patterns that really determine behavior. Studying birds and bugs, frogs, other mammals, we see that there are all kinds of patterns that invisibly dominate our behavior. Freud misses the point entirely. Species-programming, nothing to do with our individual backgrounds and personalities.

Interesting experiment with Chris this afternoon.

First watched the first scene of Massenet's *Manon*, then watched the first science of Puccini's *Manon Lescaut*. Same story, same sequence.

Young girl on her way to convent, seduced by decadent nobleman.

Only the Massenet is just *Sprachstimme* (talking), with a dull, minimal background, and the Puccini is *music*.

If you're just there for the play, then it's a very poor play. If you've got a play like *Electra*, you can do what Richard Strauss did — keep the music stark and bare, expressionistically let the play itself exude from the music.

But if you're got an inherently sappy, moralistic plot like *Manon* (the last act, Manon dying on the coastal desert of Louisiana, for example), then you've got to carry it with the music. Which Puccini does so beautifully. Even when the libretto absolutely stinks, like in his opera, what's the name of it, *George, Fred, Sam*? I forget.[8]

Chris responded, could see the difference, just couldn't put it in words.

"The one I really liked was the Italian one. Pooh... what's his name?"

"Puccini! As in Fettucini!"

---

8. The name Buckley is searching for is *Edgar*.

He had to laugh. His all-time favorite is Fettucini Alfredo at the Olive Garden.

Over to Fay's then, this afternoon, my Iranian student's daughter. Name really Shocofay.

I like the way the little girl is with Chris. He gets out of the car and slams the door, she yells at him "Don't slam the door on me that way ever again!"

And the way she does it, not really mad at all, just "just!" She's the educator, civilizer, establishes limits, patterns. And he can use it, believe me.

Amazing family. The grandfather owns orchards in Iran. Zoila (my student) is just finishing up her B.S. in Math, her husband just finishing up a Ph.D. in Chemical Engineering, her sister a Ph.D. in Math, one brother a computer whiz, the other an accountant. Everything number-related.

And Shocofay outreads Chris like the Hare versus the Tortoise.

Then into the midst of this family was born, 10 years ago, an autistic girl they call Ozzie.

My first encounter with Autism. She doesn't talk, you say hello to her and she growls. She grabs your hands, studies your fingernails with great interest, gets into the car, pries some discarded bubblegum out of the ashtray and pops it into her mouth, finds some matches and starts to eat them, goes into the refrigerator and starts eating frozen green beans, goes in circles, around and around, very graceful, very beautiful, really, dark brown, aristocratic Persian face.

Fay stays home most of the time because it's easier for Zoila to take care of Ozzie that way.

Does it seem like the world is in the hands of anyone/anything reasonable, caring, directing, when everything is pure randomness?

Shema Israel, Adonai Elohainu, Adonai Echod.
Hear, Oh, Israel, the Lord is Your God, The Lord is One.

One (random universe) God? It's more logical to be an Aztec and sacrifice victims to a hungry, cannibal Sun-God, believe in Rain-Gods and Earthquake-Gods, the four (Maya) Chacs at the four quarters of the world, a god for every minor squeak and rumble in the universe.

Like Harry, another one of Chris's friends from pre-school. Down's syndrome. And his mother is a tall, aristocratic sociologist from Kentucky, his father a Harvard Ph.D. (also sociologist), his brother a local Mozart — and there's Harry! He was in pre-school with Chris: Chris keeps developing, Harry has stopped, looks like he's even stopped growing.

To try to imagine either an eternal universe or an eternal God, you always get back to Aristotle's First Mover Itself Unmoved. First Cause. Something as far from the human mind being able to understand as a flea on the back on an elephant trying to understand it's even on an elephant, much less that the elephant is in a zoo, in a country, on a planet, in a universe. To have a personal god who cares, or even who punishes, but who KNOWS you're there, versus the Indifferent, Eternal (?) Unknowing/Unknowable...

Cried when I got off the phone with Christine tonight. Something severely, chronically wrong with her. No energy. They're talking about stenosis of the mitral valves now, septum problems, general lupus, some kind of enzyme problem. Massive, permanent, systemic problems — time to sacrifice a goat and spread its blood all over the altar to the God Who Knows and Cares (LEVITICUS).

"I'm fine as long as I don't do anything. I get out of breath just getting dressed," she said.

It's not just that she doesn't want to work — she can't. And, over the years, how much have hidden, subterranean problems contributed to her discontents and confusions and despairs and elations? What kind of chemical chaos has been sabotaging her entire life?

No money. She's coming up here on credit cards. I love her and the kids. I wish it could all come back together the way it was, just for a while — until the end. Recreate it so I could leave surrounded by the way it was.

So stupid to bring Tanya into the marriage. Haughtiness. As if it were so perfect that nothing could touch it — but it could/did.

More X-rays today. I'm getting a little burned area on my chest where the radiation's let loose.

You see all these seemingly healthy people down in the waiting room in the radiology department, a tough-ass spunky young blond guy in tight jeans, a bronzed young woman who looks like an Olympic swimmer, busy-bee old ladies full of chatter and energy. And they're all playing table-tennis with Death.

I've already lost. I know it and so does everyone else, from the receptionist to Dr. Barnes, to Mrs. Hurley, the radiation technician.

But Mrs. Hurley still goes through all the careful blocking-out of the not-to-be-treated areas, as if it meant something. Might just as well dip me in a vat of liquid lead and vaporize me. It would be kinder.

I kept listening to *Manon Lescaut* in my head. Who needs radios when you carry the stuff around in your head with you the way I do?

SATURDAY — JUNE 24
LATE NIGHT, HOT

B ought Chris Rastan for his Sega game today. Loved it for 10 minutes and then we were back to Nickelodeon again.

I asked him what was wrong and it turned out that there's one part in which you fight, not just against dragons, but Time itself. And he kept losing. Same problem with Space Harrier and even Ghost Busters. It's either an easy win or nothing.

"Come on, keep trying, you'll learn, you'll figure it out, develop skills. That's the whole point, isn't it?"

Me, my raw-nerve total twitch "nature," and then the learned, careful scholarship. Like two different me's, the Natural Disaster and the Developed Scholar.

He's such a sweetheart of a guy. He fell down by the pool today and cried, came over and sat on my lap in his wet suit. I started crying too, sitting there writing this journal, listening to Haydn's Clock Symphony, like time-travelling into another, more innocent age.

I so wanted to see Chris big — 10, 12, 21, even 32. I used to even think I'd stay teaching until he got to college and I could have him in my writing class. Like I had Margarita after the first divorce. It was such a healing experience, her seeing me in my sauce/ecological niche. I even thought maybe I'd see him married. Maybe even see his children. Thought I'd see my big books published, but it looks like I'm going to end up like the guy in James' "The Beast in the Jungle," whose special destiny was to have no special destiny, nothing at all happens to him...

Just dozed off.

It's one a.m.

I want to read a little more on the strange alignment of sacred buildings in pre-Columbian America to 285 degrees (in relation to what?) and see if I can figure out how that ultimately relates to Tiawanaku, Bolivia, which I see as the ultimate pattern-setter of building-alignments and everything else in ancient Amerindia.[9]

Let it go.

Sleep.

I've got to get the boy to his swimming lesson at 9:20. 80-85° in this room. Fan on me. I feel like the life's being drained out of me drop by drop. Only I can't find where the faucet is, much less turn it off.

SUNDAY — JUNE 25
COMMUNION

Mass this morning.

I go to Communion without going to Confession. Why not? When I think of how literally and completely I used to believe everything. And anyhow, I guess I'm pretty sinless these days.

I go because I want Chris to have 'patterns,' a religion to hang on to.

I had him baptized three years ago,and when we were down in Chicago visiting my old college chum, Frank Gazzolo, who had gone Russian Uniate (he doesn't like the term, it's the Russian Catholic Church, not Russian Orthodox) because he felt it better preserved the old traditions, Frank told me "In this church you go right to Communion after Baptism, there's no waiting around. Now you're one of the Faithful."

---

9. Buckley is referring to an article in *Archaeoastronomy in the Americas* (ed. by R.A. Williamson): "Architecture, Astronomy, and Calendrics in Pre-Columbian Meso-America," by V.H. Malstrom. He had the practice of nightly reading — as a "duty!" — something about pre-Columbian America. Sometimes, as in this case, he'd talk to me about the readings, and I'd even take notes.

Which seemed theologically sound to me so I went to Communion too — with Chris.

I made it into the Orphic Mysteries for the kid, the taking of Sacred Peyote among the Huichol Indians, magic mushrooms among the Zapotecs, Some among the ancient Hindus:

> "This is the Body and Blood of God. He dies and
> is resurrected. You eat his body and you become
> part of him, he becomes part of you..."

Which is what I used to believe in the old days in Chicago, Mass and Communion every day for 20 years. The Divine descending inside me like an egg broken, and instead of a yolk coming out, a yolklike flame. I glowed with the Godhead inside me.

I used to walk around Chicago practically levitating, luminous, numinous.

Always fasting. Singing bone.

Something to fall back on in crisis. Like when Mimi/ Christine falsely accused me of sexually molesting Chris. I couldn't quite make it back to Easter, but did manage to get to Zen. In and out of the Great Nada. Like now. My whole life now as if I'd never been.

What I want for the boy is some sense of a religion, religious community, belief, even if it is pure pie in the sky. Something to pull you through time.

Like me in the divorce trial, Christine bringing in every goddamned private, shameful thing she could about me, my pissing in the washbowl of the downstairs bathroom when I had prostate problems a few years back (always believing I'd die of prostate cancer like my Uncle Jake), because if I tried to piss in the toilet it would spray all over my pants. Or coming to the table naked in Brazil (like everyone else, which she forgot to mention), as if I were the only nudist in the tropics, the whole goddamned family walking around like a troupe of baboons. Her lawyer having at me, over and over again. Really, like the taunting of Christ.

I was supposed to blow, go berserk and lose the case that way, the crazier the better. But somehow I almost got to enjoy watching her beat the shit out of me. Curiosity at her technique, I guess. Taking a beating. Holding my own. And then bouncing back.

The relationship between religion and toughing it out?!
Losing it.

I just closed my eyes and I was off the coast of Florida looking for underwater ruins, going further and further down, slope into the Deep, darker and darker.

What was I saying, that religion is learning how to take a beating? That's what it sounds like.

And it's true. In a way that's what saved me, always feeling inside the system, like Aztec victims going to have their chests cut open, happily carrying messages to the gods.

Lord knows, Chris's mother is the total Outsider and the girls have had a big dose of that too. Amy one year of high school actually in school, the rest by correspondence. I just wonder if she'll ever make it back into the fold of normality. And the crazy-gene sliding through the DNA strands of the whole family like a random curse.

Which is a problem thinking like an old mystic. Benedict Joseph Labre was turned down by the Cistercians and the Benedictines and ended up dying, ostensibly a bum, in the streets of Paris, but no Cistercians nor Benedictines were declared saints during his century — and he was. So the Outsider becomes the farthest inside that you can get. My attraction for Christine = her "outsiderness?"

What am I saying, that Catholicism taught me how to be a good victim? What's that book by Bettelheim about surviving Auschwitz? Learning to function in the midst of institutionalized sadism? That's what the court was for me, my Auschwitz. But I didn't crack. I guess I'd learned the Way of the Cross, the Way of the Crucifixion. And Benedict Jose Labre wasn't ever really "outside" Catholicism, had his own inner Catholic integrity. Maybe that's what I want Chris to learn from Catholicism as institution — how to reject the institution whenever it betrays itself, and find integrity inside yourself.

I guess ultimately I see Christine as a Holy Outsider. Like Mauriac's *Thérèse*.

Watched *Billy Liar* this afternoon. The boy simply refused to watch it, goofed around, let Aziza the hair-hound loose, and she jumped all over the couch and him, and his black Batman shirt ended up looking like a blond porcupine. Then he went out on the porch, got out the hose, Aziza got out, I had to go out with a hamburger patty and lure her home. Finally he watched a little of the film, this Mr. Nobody in the England Midlands, Mr. Nobody in the middle of Nowhere, always talking about going to London, who creates a private universe in his own head where he's general, dictator, hero. In a way it's Chris himself, inside his own video-game universe, where he either has to always win or he flips it off.

Actually *listening* to him today.

We get up, he asks: "What day is it?"

I tell him Sunday.

"Do we have to go to swimming class?"

"No, on Sunday we go to church."

"Do we have to go?"

"Yes, we have to go..."

No sense of schedule, always trying to bypass whatever *is* scheduled. The boy's mind is like a dish of scrambled eggs. Even at eight, just on the nether-side of normal. And as he gets older?

Brunch over at The Club. Then Chris went swimming with Tanya. He's actually learning how to swim. A major breakthrough.

Called Christine from the poolside phone. I don't/can't swim, of course.

She detailed the situation in Kansas City. Father back in the hospital. Aseptic, isn't that the word? Systemic infection — after 3 operations for aortic aneurisms, another one for bladder problems. It's not cancer but still a cellular problem, his whole mesothelium/connective tissue just breaking up, disintegrating. And Christine's mother has some problem with clotting in her legs. Her lungs shot. Genetically related to Christine's own lung problem.

It gets her down.

"All I do is chauffeur around the dying; it's almost like driving a hearse all day."

Watching the whole thing run down. Familial entropy.

She'd just been out cutting the lawn when I called. Resting afterwards.

"Doing anything just wipes me out, even getting dressed."

"You can't imagine how much I miss you," I say, "I'll tell you the truth, I don't think couples like us happen very often."

And for a moment she listened, accepted it; it was like pouring sacramental wine into the chalice of our lives, both of us somehow discarding the whole divorce trial, all the sexual molestation bullshit as tactics and games. Fucking Mimi! You know it was all from her!

Mimi's down in Texas visiting her family, so Christine's loose for a change, unmoored, floating in a sea of her own selfness.

Christine is the great mimic. When she met me I was a Man of Letters so she became a Woman of Letters, actually wrote a book of poetry that got published by Barn Sparrow

Press in Wichita. Poems about her dead grandmother, mainly. Her grandmother had been the center of sanity in her young life, the same way my grandmother had been the center of sanity in mine.

I remember when I first started going down to Kansas City, the grandmother would save up articles for me on archaeology.

"Just a few things I cut out of newspapers and magazines," she'd say, and hand me a whole envelope of stuff.

The kitchen, the house, was her cosmos. She'd sit and talk about the old days in Texas and Oklahoma, putting in the railroads, building up the towns, filling the emptiness, always living inside a global sense of history, always reading the newspaper, always watching the news on TV, oracular, sibylline, white-haired, hunched-over sanity. As a counterweight to Mr. Grump in the living room.

I remember one time Nina telling me that she was in the bathroom washing, about 12 years old, just developing breasts, and her father had opened the bathroom door, saw her and went berserk.

"What's wrong with you? Cover yourself up!"

And he was the one who had opened the door into her privacy. Welcome to puberty!

Totally humorless, a Nordic, Northman mind that never could have come out of the Magna Mater sanity of the Mediterranean.

Lecome Du Noüy (Human Destiny) was right, there is a passing-down of traits through human history, not just genetically, but in terms of familiar conditioning. Christine's father's influence spreads out into the history of the family like a cancer. And the mother's cooperating with the whole dictatorship didn't leave Christine with any model for easy options. It was either bow her head and take the blow (like her mother) or run away and hide (as if she were still three

years old) — no adult coping-mechanisms. Evil and collabora-
tors with Evil.

I come into the bedroom at eleven/eleven-fifteen, Chris
is reading one of the Babar the Elephant books. He's reading
well.

They were calling him dyslexic down in Kansas, were all
set to send him to a special school.

But I think what had happened to him was that he'd
been infected by the virus of family malaise too.

The surprise-attack divorce, him seeing me go down
when I found Christine and Mimi out at Mimi's place and
approached the car. "What are you doing in town, I thought
you were down in Kansas? Christine behind the wheel. Mimi
screamed "Hit it!" (Or was it "Hit him!"?). And Christine
took off, I started running next to the car, she swerved, I
went down, my right arm fractured, Chris's agonized face in
the back of the car looking at me go down — as they drove
off. Tanya came over, helped me up, drove me down to
Sparrow Hospital, all night in surgery, metal plates holding the
pieces together for a year, then another surgery to take the
metal out. I have all the hardware in a little plastic contained
on the dresser in my bedroom. It must weigh a pound.

And that was only one incident in a whole hysterical way
of life, leaving town and then down to Chicago, hiding, no
address, no phone number, then they wanted child-support
so they had to surface again, twice as much as they were
supposed to get, then triple, always more, surfacing more, re-
establishing normality on the basis of how much I was
willing/able to pay for it.

Let's not call Chris dyslexic but INFECTED.

I kiss Chris and Tanya, practically crawl into my room.

As I lay me down to sleep, I pray the Lord my soul to
keep.

I wouldn't be surprised at all if one of these mornings I simply don't wake up.

WEDNESDAY, JUNE 28
CHRISTINE I, II, III.

*C*hristine arrived last night, came to the house at midnight. Amy knocked on my door. I was sitting on my bed reading letters between Pasternak, Marina Tsvetayeva and Rilke, Summer of 1926, listening to Bruckner's 9th. Letters written while Rilke was dying.

Amy comes into the room.

"They're downstairs."

For a moment I don't know who "they" are.

And there they were, in the living room.

Christine's a little overweight, a little more wrinkled around the eyes, but otherwise unchanged.

Funny the lukewarmness, even negativity, I feel toward her. Or worse than that — fear. For all my forgiving. At the deepest levels you never forgive or forget. Again conditioning. I look at the doughy white middle-aged flesh and can't even imagine her as the wild, lycra sex-cat who wanted it five times a night every night.

How can you love and then so violently un-love? Because the *you* changes. There was Christine I, the lace unitard SCREAM, then along came Dillinger-Mimi, and Christine II, the amoral character-killer, was born and started to munch cupcakes and peanut brittle.

Something inside me so very reluctant to trust her even a little, even now...

For me her desperate need for sex, her oiled, pneumatic flesh under the stretch-lace, finally had brought me incarnated out of the world of the eternal Gothic greystone Word. I became "real." That was the great tragedy, her greatest crime — to have betrayed the depth/completeness of our love that sprang out of our flesh like vast, tropical leaves.

I think of our past together, and I think casseroles, napkin holders, clean sheets, enormous pillows, freshly squeezed orange juice, bubble baths, you open a drawer and it smells of lilac, you get into bed and it smells simply clean.

Twyla sitting on the sofa next to her mom.

"Twyla doesn't feel 'right' about staying here," says Christine legalistically, "so we're going to the University Inn on Trowbridge."

Of course, Amy is staying in her room. It's all fixed up now. New drapes, comforter, pillows. She was here all Winter and Spring, she's home.

And I can understand Twyla's feelings too — if they really are *her* feelings. After the divorce she lived with me for almost a year, then on the final day of the divorce-proceedings, Christine dipped into the Law and *took her away against her will.* They kept her out of school for a couple years. Home almost full-time, took her to some social worker who had never even met me, who told her that, yes, I had sexually molested her brother. Which, I think, pulled the rug right out from under her psychologically. I had always been kind of the rock of her sanity, her best pal.

With Mimi always in the Control Room manipulating everything that was going on on stage. The Gorgon/Medusa. I've never seen eyes like that in anyone else's head. Loves courts, loves to (mis)use the law against you. Tall, all wrinkled-up, only in her forties, but already looks like something you'd dig up in a Nazca grave.

It's such a knot to untie. I can hardly even get it straight in my memory. As if there's not one Christine, but multiple, good-evil, black-white, and all the shades in between, Christines!

They were all working in the same lab, Futuro Tech — Tanya, Christine and Mimi. Christine had come to the conclusion that she was homosexual and wanted another woman. Only Tanya, although she'd been playing around with Christine just to prove she could, wasn't really homosexual. So I suggested (like the naïve fool I am) that Christine simply find another woman.

The Great Rationalist: "Why break structures. We don't have to get a divorce, none of these legal games really fit the human condition anyhow."

And there was Mimi — the lone Jackal/Hyena. So they paired up, and Mimi did a crazy thing — the thing, I think, that's the key to the whole war that followed.

Mimi is totally divorced from any of the "normal" human needs and comforts, physical and psychological. She's hardwood floors instead of pillows, burlap instead of velour, the hard march instead of the long sleep. Warrior Woman. It's all money, success, or (even more than that) THE GAME/ THE WAR. Like if Hitler could have only gotten "comfortable," had a few more beers and started taking long afternoon naps...

Futurotech, where they were working, was engaged in longevity research, and Mimi stole some of the cells she'd developed in her part of the research. She was found out, accused of Grand Larceny (along with Christine), and Tanya was brought in as a witness for the prosecution, and she testified that, yes, Mimi and Christine had mislabelled certain sets of cells they were working on, and later these cells, and no other cells, were "missing."

In fact, I asked Christine in the middle of the divorce-process exactly why she was getting the divorce, and she told me: "I think like a Mafioso. Tanya broke the Code, and I'm taking Chris away from her forever."

Only to take him away from Tanya, they had to destroy ME. Hence the whole strategy of accusing me of sexually molesting the boy, and all the consequences that that entailed — cops, lie-detectors, lawyers, judges...

So family, home, love, sex, all became subordinated to the War Games. Mimi's whole mind operated like Operation Desert Storm, and, in fact, she was forever reading books about Rommel and World War II, Hitler and his other generals, tactics, strategies.

Life was nothing without the Game.

Now Mimi was in Texas for six weeks and Christine was reverting back to a whole other type.

Over at the University Club much of the day, just sitting around, and there was one point when Maria del Carmen, my first wife, Bab's mother, was over at the far end of the pool doing laps, and Tanya and Christine were a few feet from me (at the pool edge) in the pool playing with Christopher. My three wives, the last three and a half decades of my life, all in the pool together.

Brian Junior down at the University of Texas working on his Ph.D. in Math, Margarita in Farmington Hills, Babs, Twyla... what if they'd all been there.

Christine in a black, old lady's swimsuit, with a skirt yet, a black sex-panther turned into a black hippo; Tanya still wickedly compact in a tiger-skin lycra bathing suit; Amy all sleek in gold and white; Twyla in a red cotton suit with a little ballet-skirt ruffle, kind of echoing her mother. Skinny little wet-puppy Chris forever in the pool, the women in and out, getting cokes, swimming, then hamburgers and fries, me sitting there in an incongruously preppy seersucker suit, barely hanging on to the day, counting the hours, the minutes, the breaths, *adieu, adieu, do I wake or dream*, that's how I really feel all the time now, like Rilke's last letters to Marina Tsvetayeva, dying of leukemia, talking about a vague "heaviness" settled permanently over him. The sentences get lost on the page, everything dissolves for long, glacial moments, and then refocuses.

I was thinking that if anyone had taken a picture (still or video) of us at poolside and carefully analyzed it, analyzed the words, postures, anything, there would be only one conclusion they could come to: *Yes, these are people who have been and who always will be cemented together for life.*

And then you add: *But they were never smart enough to figure it out, or humble enough to admit it.*

THURSDAY, JUNE 29

Twyla's birthday today.
Fifteen.
She's over her misgivings about the house now. They left the University Inn this morning and she's moved back into her room upstairs next to mine, Amy and Christine are in Amy's room downstairs. Christine's not about to move back into the same bed with Tanya — but almost.

I came into the kitchen today, back from the park with Chris, and they were sitting there as if the last five years hadn't even passed — talking about me.

Just heard fragments as I came in (a little too slow and quietly, I guess) through the dining room.

The burning question.

How long do I have. Nothing about what are my chances, just WHEN.

I didn't even ask them about Chris staying, in fact almost feel like letting loose, opening my hands and letting it all just go. You get to a point when you almost want it to end. Like William Carlos Williams' mother's last words: "I'm bored by trees."

But still, I loved just sitting by the pool today in the sun — like a lizard.

I wrote "lizard" and in my mind I saw a wall full of sunning lizards. Northern Brazil. João Pessoa, Fortaleza, what, 20 years ago? Then, thinking about the lizards, and a whole grab-bag of puzzle-pieces was dumped on the floor of my mind. Machu Picchu and the whole Urubamba River Valley, looking up at the green humps/tumuli/buttes surrounding me like giant green ghosts as I walked by the river, and then in the distance the snow-capped Andes.

The oasis of San Pedro de Atacama in Chile. You stand there and look out at the snow-capped volcanos.   Or the train from Chile to Bolivia. How many sun-gates like that at Tiawanaku did I see off in the distance? All simple pastoralism now, and no one understands the autocratic structures that once reigned here (the way I do) — the dynasty of Tiawanakan sun-kings that the Incas, thousands of years later, imitated.

It's as if I carry a thousand lives with me into oblivion.

Do I believe in the resurrection of the body and life everlasting? A personal God who is following this whole progression into death? Or is it all just dem bones, dem bones, dem dry bones, in a mindless desert of eternal "forces"?

Twyla's birthday party over at The Club.   The waiters and waitresses all came around and sang happy birthday. She seems too tall and striking now, all the baby-fat, chunkiness gone, the swan finally sliding along on the black waters of her own destiny.   That's how I saw her tonight, like a swan.

I saw Chang, this Gay Chinese former friend of Twyla's, over at Meijer's today. He's going to the Art Institute in Chicago in the Fall. All this loopy, doopy, goofy, shaggy punk force moving toward some sort of Andy Warholish self-definition.

I *believe* in the kid. I wish I could believe a little more in Twyla's direction and future.

For the last 3-4 years I've paid her to do covers for my little poetry mag, EGG-BEATER. Abstract, powerful, weird. Eyes with roots sprouting out of the ends and retina, lamp-posts with women's heads where the lamps ought to be, floating women with three heads and lots of hair and robes. Dali, Chagall, Magritte.

Only underneath the genius... she talks a lot about things closing in. "You never know what to expect, maybe it's something in me." So much paranoia, agoraphobia, depression here and there and everywhere in the family. And it seems to really surface in your late teens, early twenties.

*****

Took Chris into my room tonight, showed him the plastic boxes of cassettes I'd made for him during the years when he wasn't around, when I'd see him in terms of hours a year instead of days or months.

"I've got the whole Ring Cycle for you — music plus commentary. All you have to do is follow the numbers — *Siegfried* I, II, III, etc. *Die Götterdämmerung* I, II, III... I've done the same for *La Bohème, Turandot, Tosca, Carmen, the Magic Flute*, Mahler's *Das Lied von der Erde*. There's a whole wall of stuff. You're too young for it now, it doesn't mean anything to you, but I'm going to ask Tanya to keep it for you until you're older, maybe fifteen, eighteen. I actually enjoy listening to the tapes now. Maybe you'll have to be fifty before they really grab you. Like Bruckner. I hated Bruckner's 9th symphony for years. Too pompous, too directionless, just trivial meanderings. I thought! And then in the last few years I began to respond to it. Just the chords. The configurations, shapes, tones of the chords. Like a touch of tarragon in roast chicken."

I want(ed) so much to see him THEN, grown, see how this whole thing turns out.

Babs is so depressing. The weight. The smell. She'll be in bed until 2 p.m. every day. No reason to get up or change clothes or shower. And then she'll call:

"I just had a grilled cheese sandwich on rye bread with caraway seeds and a thick, crispy crust, and a tomato salad with *Thousand Island* dressing on it, and two glasses of fruit-punch, and a bag of barbecue-flavored Fritos, and..."

Back in California when she was a kid I'd take her to piano lessons every week with my old friend from Chicago, Murray Bradshaw, who had been the organist in the church I went to all during college — Our Lady of Peace on south 79th Street.

He was working on his Ph.D. in Musicology at UCLA.

What a coincidence — that continuity I live for.

And every Sunday I'd take the kids to concerts, no different from the way I am now, the same message, the same intensity, and the end-result is Today's Special. Eat and sleep, sleep and eat. She ought to be in a hospital somewhere, not in her mother's basement. She ought to be bathed and taken care of. Her mother ought to have someone come in and wash her clothes every week, give her a bath.

It's like Zoila, my Iranian student, and her autistic daughter, Ozzie.

I was driving down the street today and I saw them walking along over by St. Thomas Aquinas Church (where Chris was baptized). Before she saw me, I got a good look at her face. A woman on fire. On the rack. In despair. Hanging on. I could almost read her thoughts: *Why has this happened to me, why?*

Then she saw me, smiled, was her normal, social self again.

Pen all over the page. 1:30 a.m., a little cool breeze coming in over my naked body. Can hardly breathe, phlegm, congestion, the space occupied by the tumor itself. I can feel it, like an angry, clenched fist (La Raza!) inside my chest.

FRIDAY, JUNE 30
LAST CLASS & FAREWELL PARTY

T anya took off the day today, and she and Christine and the girls took Chris over to swimming class. I slept in until eleven, then got up, got dressed and walked over to class. Stopped off to get my mail first, my boss called me in, told me point-blank, "I think it's time to just stop, don't you?"

She's a blond English terrier of a woman, married to a mainland Chinese mathematician. No sharp edges. Just aggressive straightforwardness and concern.

"I wouldn't mind."

"I can just take the rest of the classes for you. Fill in. If you've got a syllabus... you can give me a little run-down as to what you've been doing."

"O.K.," I said, reaching into the Bolivian leather bag (with a little "insert" of Andean weaving sewn into a front panel, rows of sun symbols all over it.)

Handed her the syllabus, a copy of the anthology of contemporary U.S. poets I've been working on for 4-5 years, with the idea of eventually seeing it into print.

Nice red plastic cover, thick, plastic spiral binding.

Title: *Other Messages*.

Poets like Lifshin, Beining, Stanley Nelson, Todd Moore, Millie Mae Wicklund, John Bennett, John M. Bennett...

A lot of them poets I've published in EGG-BEATER.

"They're writing essays about anyone in the anthology."

"O.K., that's straightforward enough," then embarrassed. Not her strong points, empathy and compassion. "And listen... I'm dreadfully sorry," shaking hands, "I suppose you ought to do today's class anyhow, goodbyes and all that."

I don't even want to know about all the departmental discussions that have preceded this. Nothing spontaneous about anything that goes on around here. Nothing.

"Thanks."

One more brief, hanging moment, and I was gone.

*****

Of course, the whole way over I felt like I was floating rather than walking, floating into the office, over to my mailbox. Two poems just out in SLIPSTREAM, a letter from Lynne Savitt with pictures from our trip to her place. I looked (past tense) so deceptively young and healthy.

Of course, this is the only way to do it.

It's going so fast I can't believe it.

No one had papers again today. Began with 30, down to 20 now, and only 15 there. The usual summer-school problems. Everybody fucks off. What kinds of grades do they expect, I don't know. And I suppose it's me too. There's just so much you can take of professors on fire in front of you.

So I ended up talking about Bukowski again. Fake bum, fake alcoholic. At 69 much more image than reality.

Role-playing. Mask created out of Baudelaire, Rimbaud, Poe, Hemingway, Hamsun, Van Gogh, Toulouse-Lautrec.

The Outsider, L'Étranger.

Not that it's not real to some extent for Bukowski, but the reality of his childhood — Ham and Rye, Memories of a Dirty Old Man — and even his adulthood — Post Office — have little to do with the myth.

I talked a little about Bukowski's father. The Great Negator. Like Christine's father. You'd think the kids would get annihilated, but they don't, they just get twisted into permanent Outsiders. If you're not comfortable with yourself, how can you ever fit in ANYWHERE?!

I talked about how Bukowski hated me as the symbol of the fair-haired boy with the silver spoon in his mouth, but like A.D. Winans said in a recent letter to me, Bukowski makes the mistake of supposing that his kind of pain is the ONLY pain. What about my two divorces and six tortured kids, a Godzilla Mom, Marshmallow Monster Dad, no brothers or sisters? And now death at 57?

Invited the class over for the evening. One jackass asked: "What's the point of the party? What are we going to do?"

"It's a farewell party," I answered. "Margaret Thatcher Regina is taking over for me."

"What I really had in mind was a little warm blood for Twyla — and Amy. Twyla's especially starving for people. She feels totally out of it down on the edge of Kansas City, told me today, "I don't fit in with anybody down there, they're all such a bunch of hicks."

Especially out where they are, the equivalent of the slum rings around the major cities of Latin America (I'm thinking especially of Lima). Only in Kansas it's not so much materially as intellectually/spiritually impoverished.

Lunch at Olga's. My (our) Visa. Christine always acts as if money were infinite. And then Chris and the girls walked over by the river to feed the ducks, and Tanya, Christine and I were left by ourselves, very neatly all pre-choreographed.

CHRISTINE: Tanya and I both agree, we think I ought to take Chris back to Kansas with me. If she wasn't working and had all day to help out with the boy... but as it is, it's just too much for you to handle.

TANYA: You may have to move into the hospital soon.

ME: What the fuck is that supposed to mean?

TANYA: I was talking to Dr. Hermann this morning. Or I should say he was talking to me.

ME: And?

TANYA: We can go into details tonight. I can bring home the latest X-rays.

ME (feeling ironically that I'd just flunked an exam, my final orals for the Ph.D., something like that. My ultimate reference-point — final exams): How soon are you leaving?

CHRISTINE: Monday.

ME: O.K.

I got up. "I'll be back at the house," handed Tanya the Visa card, walked home, up to my room.

The whole bookshelf full of tapes for the boy.

So many years without him. *The Ring, Tosca*, Strauss's *Elektra*, Berg's *Wozzeck*. I thought he'd especially like *Wozzeck* with all his love for the grotesque, that part where Wozzeck, after he murders his sweetheart, goes into the bloody water of the lake where he's thrown the body, and the music turns into pure nightmare. Walking out into the water scream-singing:

Das Wasser ist Blut /The water is blood.

Berg would have been great for horror-movie scores like *Friday the 13th*, the *Nightmare on Elm Street* films.

And then the art videos I'd bought at the Metropolitan Museum in New York — Chagall, Magritte, Goya...

I want that eight-year-old to be ten today, twelve tomorrow, 38 by Monday.

I wanted him to sit in/soak up my writing classes, I wanted to go to the Dordogne in Spring with him, prehistoric-man territory, the woods still full of memories of hairy rhinoceroses and mammoths and careful Neanderthal burials, covering the corpse with prayers and carefully-selected wild flowers.

I wanted to take the boy to Lagoa Santa/Holy Lagoon in Brazil, the most controversial site in the New World, re-look at whatever skull "evidence" is left at the university in Bela Horizonte. All part of a book I wanted to write against Hridlicka, the Ivan the Terrible of Amerindian anthropology, who suppressed whatever evidence that surfaced that conflicted with his far-right theories about the relative recentness of man in the so-called New World.

I wanted to take the boy to Tiawanaku, Machu Picchu, Pisac, Ollantaytambo, all my sacred sites in the Andes, and then go to Easter Island, across the Pacific to the Tonga Islands, to the Indus Valley sites, Mohenjo Daro, Harappa. Then to Carthage (Tunis).

I'm four years away from retirement (at 61), and I had been thinking of taking off maybe Spring and Summer during my 60's, taking the boy to Vienna or Berlin, Barcelona. Bum around in the Uffizi in Florence — the Botticellis, Della Robbias... doing his schoolwork by correspondence...

The languages. Six months in Austria, and he could get an idea of the worst of possible German dialects, then up to Frankfurt for the real thing.

So full of projections and extrapolations. And now it's all cut down. Brahms's *German Requiem: Wir sind wie Grass/* We are like grass. And now it's all cut down and burned.

Party tonight. Luis Wassman came, a couple others. Most never showed, but Wassmann brought the next editor of THE RED CEDAR REVIEW, a Palestinian Arab filmmaker who looked like an Orthodox Jew, a reporter for the STATE NEWS. And Twyla was in her glory.

They talked about film-making, about Wim Wenders, Almadovar, the latest (Spanish) rage, about Chantal Ackermann, the Warhol diaries, about going to UCLA, about going to Berlin, here, there, everywhere, kinetic, pure energy.

Just the way I used to be in my twenties. We'd go and see something like T.S. Eliot's *The Cocktail Party*, Christopher Fry's *The Lady's Not For Burning*, Racine's *Phèdre*, and then afterwards go over to Berghoff's and drink beer and talk for hours. Not that there was that much to talk about in *The Cocktail Party*. Or Cocteau, he was another big gadfly/mystery-man for us — *Orpheus, The Eternal Return*. And whatever happened to the Neo-Shakespearianisms of Christopher Fry? I used to like him, like him a lot.

Anyhow, the party worked for Twyla. She was fascinated, intrigued, in her juice, the way she used to be in the middle of Punkdom right here in this town.

After they left, she told me "I wish I was back here. I really liked that Luis."

"His mother's Nicaraguan, his father German, there's some kind of import-export business in Miami, he's always talking about going to Berlin to study filmmaking. He's an interesting star to hitch on to. And so are you!"

"I just feel so ignorant."

"You're not ignorant, you're just beginning."

Wanting to see her (too) at her zenith, 15, 25, 35...

The Pleiades above the moon this morning. It's so easy to see how ancient myth formed: *The seven-headed dragon descended upon the pale goddess...*

Let it go, let it go, my whole being says. Want to read a little about solstice observation-sites in Chaco Canyon. I remember Robert Louis Stevenson writing about some

Chinese scholar who used to put mosquitos inside the sleeves of his shirt so they'd bite him awake. That's what I need.

SATURDAY — JULY 1
BRUCKNER, EXTENDED CHORDS

Slept in all morning. The disease doesn't progress steadily but capriciously/capricornishly. Like a goat. I'll feel *up* for hours, and then suddenly it drops out from under me like the belly of a plane opening, and I fall — parachuteless — out.

They all went out to the mall to screw around, brought me back some fig bars from GNC, Amy all hot about some black leather stuff she wanted to buy — skirts, jackets. She came home at dawn from Frank's. Christine told me she told her to stay overnight instead of coming home in the wee hours. The only thing I worry about is AIDS. After Todd Lawson's death, it became so much more real for me. Now comes Medical Neo-Puritanism, like it or not.

Chris came into my room after they got back. I was listening to Bruckner's 9th. The obstinate, ostinato power of all those little fragments of his building toward climaxes, and the power of the big-punch chords. You wouldn't think you could get so much pleasure out of just the right manipulation of intervals.

Chris seemed to catch onto/get hooked by the music. I remembered years ago when the Vienna Philharmonic was at the Wharton Center here and Bruckner's 9th was on the program, and *Gone With the Wind* on the TV at the same time, Amy fought me, wanted to just forget about the concert — to hell with my season tickets. I remembered how Jennifer, one of Christine's friends, had videotaped *Gone With the Wind* for Amy, and that's why we ended up getting our first VCR. Electronic archaeology.

Bruckner never heard this symphony performed. And even after his death, the first performances "normalized" the music, got rid of all the jagged edges and eccentric chords. This is the original version. Von Karajan and the Berlin Philharmonic.

Chris actually sat down on the bed and listened, his eyes straying around the walls covered with mementos of my life: A discarded, never-used cover for *Head* by Jim Kay, the sun coming out of a man's mouth like a molten cannonball — the final cover had substituted a butterfly for the sun, a much weaker design-idea, I'd thought. A poem by Larry Kopf I'd gotten out of the wastebasket at his place, all about his wife's cancer — he's Orpheus and she's Eurydice in a radioactive cobalt underworld. Some drawings by my old Argentinean buddy, Edgardo Antonio Vigo — a big comic-book-style pop-art gun pointing out into the room. Title: *Urbanus!* A self-taken photo of Blythe Ayne in the middle of a forest dressed in voluminous folds of white lace, dancing, the photo all "worked over" so that all you can see, really, is a flurry of white lace and a white silhouette of a face against the dark forest backdrop. A framed poem by William Wantling, dead, I don't know, a decade or more, signed *Remember, we were lost in time together.* As if I could forget him. A picture of Lynne Savitt ten years ago, blonde, bronzed, in a red satin corset, her black eyes looking hungry and poodleish. A concrete poem signed by the English Concretist John Furnivall, a Statue of Liberty all made out of words. The piles of manuscripts all over my desk, on shelves all over the room. Most of my life right there in front of me.

The boy just sat and looked. I remember when he was a baby and his mother and Tanya would be in my bed with him, he'd say: "Daddy, type, it puts me to sleep."

I wonder where I went wrong as a writer. The value they stressed most in grad school was ORIGINALITY. Like Woolf, Joyce, Faulkner, even Kerouac — the unmistakable voice-print. Which I think I had. Only everyone wanted the exact opposite. Generic sameness. Flatness. Agents would tell me: "Read the best-seller list, forget the bullshit, leave the experiments for chemistry."

Christine had come into my life epileptically withered, like an old tree-canker, carrying rheumy-eyed, tooth-picking fathers and hatchet-wielding grandfathers and maiden aunts who smelled like old photo albums in mouldy basements, grandmothers and mothers filled with echoing Prussian Hessian field orders. She opened her mouth and you could hear Das Volk echoing out across the fields of killer-hunger: *Ein Volk, ein Krieg, eine Hoffnung, etwas zu essen!*

That's Christine, a thousand sluggish corrupt rivers of European decadence draining into a mindless Situationist camp.

I took the boy in my arms.

"I've never loved anyone in my life the way I love you. What I want for you is for you to know who you are, to feel good about yourself. No one systematically tore you down and convinced you you're a worthless piece of shit, which is what happened to both me and your mother. You're on track, stay on track, find a woman who likes herself too, someone who's just as on track as you are. It doesn't have to be all fucked-up. There's always tragedy. To be born is tragic in a way, but you don't have to work full-time, like most people do, to make it worse!"

Holding onto him. I like his innocent, eight-year-old smell, his shaggy hair, his softness, the way he's always good with kids. Like when we go to the little park over by Central School sometimes in the evenings, there'll be little, little kids there, and I love to watch him play with them, help them up to the various levels of the jungle gym, help them down, help them get into and out of the swings.

I always tell him: "It shows how good a father you'll be. Your mother and I always loved you, you'll pass it on, that's the way it goes. All Bukowski has to pass on is HATE because that's all he ever had in his own life."

Christine comes in, asks me if I want to go to the pool. Fine.

Tanya took off the afternoon. Vacation-time. The hospital loves it when she fractions it like that. So there we all were together again. I swear, with Mimi out of the way in Texas, out of the picture entirely, Christine back here, it's like getting in the old Time Machine and going back five years, *ménage a trois* in the Grand (familial) Manner. And it's a funny thing about East Lansing, probably because it's a college town: nobody ever said a word.

Rented *Vision Quest*, but nobody liked it. Too much quest and not enough vision. Who the fuck but an anthropologist like me even knows what a vision-quest is?

Then I went over to Pistachio's and bought a big loaf of multi-grained, rough, primitive, peasant bread, got some amaretto-flavored coffee and German wild-berry preserves over at Castellani's, and we had one of our old-time bread and jelly feasts.

That's all we used to concentrate on in the old days — fluffy, flowered comforters and cotton tops and tights, cashew and almond butter, guava, quince, gooseberry preserves, different kinds of cheeses and differed flavored coffees, and Christine was always a bright purple and russet and green cotton-clothed goddess in rough leather sandals or rough suede boots, and then the three of us would go into my room, on to my big bed, and the beautiful madness would begin.

Christine so much wanted me to get Tanya pregnant. It was going to be their, our, all three of ours, child. Chris, and then Baby X. Only with all the fertility-cycle charts and sperm tests in the world, it never happened. I'd always "insert" into Tanya, and then the two women would go at it together for another hour while I lay back against the wall and half-watched, half-dozed. You can't blame Christine for thinking that sex with Tanya was permanent. That's sure the way it looked.

To see Christine now, sickish and bloated, with her obstinate, repetitive business about Mimi and the Current Project. Now it's AIDS, as if the two of them are going to slay the dragon that all God's armies have been trying to slay for years. The "spark" gone out of her, old lady...

Although, in the kitchen, under the tapered little candle-light-like lights in the huge, hexagonal, colored-glass bird case of a light-fixture that I'd brought back from Valencia in 1976, the room alive with coffee- and bread- and jelly-smells, the two girls, Chris, Tanya, it was like a Rembrandt, Hals, Titian, all the rich chiaroscuro vibrato of a Renaissance kitchen immortalized.

And I had all I could do to keep from breaking down. I was the one, after all, who had suggested to Christine: "If you want, feel you really need another woman, why don't you simply find one," breaking the bond, instead of holding on to her forever, "du, du, du allein," setting her adrift.[10]

And how adrift can you get? Feeling for long moments that in that kitchen filled with soft orange and white light, that it was all back in place, restored, Lazarus come back from the

---

10. *Du, du, du allein* ("You, you, you alone") — from a Kreisler song about Vienna.

dead for dinner, the Prodigal Son returned: "The lost has been recovered, the dead returned to life."

Then alone up to my room, everyone else downstairs watching TV, listening to the Bruckner with earphones, letting the music carry me out into Spaceship Night, feeling that one more moment and I'd be inside the Mind of God, the She-kinah waiting for all eternity to be awakened...[11]

Chris comes in, lies down with me. I put the earphones on him, he puts his head back, just listening, listening, starting to cry.

My breathing sounds like a file filing a rusty bar now, like someone sandpapering down a table leg. It's becoming such an effort to just breathe. All night long I felt that I was already mostly gone, just one thin bloody chickengut scrap of fiber holding me down to life and Earth at all.

SUNDAY — JULY 2
BEAUTIFUL WOMEN

B runch at The Club, of course, today. Everyone in gala. Me and four beautiful women, and then the little boy.

I always liked the idea of being with beautiful women/a beautiful woman. Like the old days in Chicago when I'd take Dolores Volini to Orchestra Hall every Saturday night. Box seats. Me and my lady. Her always caped and draped and coiffured, flowing, flowing, textured, blacks and dark reds and deep purples. But when it came time to get serious with her she wouldn't have me, which set my life on a whole different (and disastrous) trajectory.

---

11. A Kaballistic reference to the female part of the Godhead.

Christine came into my room not more than an hour ago. I had my earphones on, local drugstore reading glasses, miniature score of Bruckner's 9th in hand (always amused at these tiny scores for monumental symphonic structures), fun to see on paper the structure of the triumphant-Frankenstein chords.

"You really take this shit seriously, don't you?"

"I should have gone into the business," I answered.

Would have, I suppose, if my father hadn't pushed me into Medicine after a total childhood in music and the other arts. And then, when I dropped out of Medicine, it was so much easier for me to get a Ph.D. in English instead of a Ph.D. in Music/Musicology. I'd left music behind for so many years. So to catch up again...

"Don't talk to me about 'should-haves,' that's the story of my life," she half-smiled.

Earphones off. One light over my bed. The eyes of the dragon masks on the wall or hanging from the ceiling, all staring out from the bundled shadows. It's killer hot, I've got a fan full on me, I'm stretched out naked on the bed.

"I want to talk to you about taking Chris back to Kansas City with me. I've decided — Tanya and I have decided — to leave him here a little longer. I don't want to cut anything short. You're still functioning, I don't want to take anything away from you that's yours, at the same time I don't want him to suffer needlessly."

Letting it end in a knot of ambiguity. Define *needlessly*, what does that mean? There's no point in having him see his father slip noisily into Death's Dream Kingdom?

"Listen, about us," I start to say.

All this monumental ambiguity about HER/HER NATURE. How can you have three children with a man, pass fifteen unfailingly orgasmic years with him, and then all of a sudden go GAY? As if it were predetermined, inevitable, no choice involved.

Todd Lawson and his specialized sexuality so different.

"All that turns me on," he'd always tell me, "is Chinese guys under 25." We'd sit around talking in San Francisco bars, and he'd see some young Chinese guy walk by and react, "Look at that tight ass!"

And even then I'd wonder how much was really instinct and how much self-programming. And Christine, a thousand times more intellectualized. Like adopting a Code, a Creed, like becoming a Nazi or a radical Christian:

I BELIEVE IN WOMAN, THE FORCE ETERNAL,
AND DISBELIEVE IN THE PUNY MALE.
ALL MY ENERGY, MY LIFE, MY DREAMS
SHALL BE DEVOTED TO THE WORSHIP
OF THE YONI.

Like Siva phallic worship in India. I remember when I was on a Fulbright in Madras and one day Maria del Carmen and I walked into this saivite temple, a huge stone phallus in the middle of the temple and women going up and caressing, praying to it, "oiling it" with melted butter.

It all seems so fake to me — for her.

"Listen, about us," I start to say, and all the soft, compassionate defenselessness is suddenly replaced by the Warrior Woman again.

"Us, except as parents, is *past tense!*"

And she's up and out with a "see you in the morning" trailing after her like a shredded purple chiffon tail.

I won't sleep at all tonight. All these adrenalin-like chemicals being produced by my cancer-cells themselves, the day so full of promise, and now the night swings shut again like a bank vault.

Brunch, then the pool, the languorously hot, tropical, festive afternoon. I drive out to North Park, and then in the evening a performance of Euripides' *The Trojan Women* down at the Sun Bowl by the City Market, across the river from Consumer's Power, giant smoke stacks towering up in the background — a great backdrop for the fall of Troy.

The Fall of Consumer's Power!

Floating full-time, hanging on. I couldn't remember who Helen's lover was or where she was or why this or why that, my memory getting to be like an old illegible gravestone. You know someone's buried there, but you don't know who or for how long.

MONDAY — JULY 3
SHE'S GONE

Then Christine and the girls left early this morning. I got up to see them off, Chris still asleep up in his bed in the little half-room next to Tanya.

I can't even say that I really slept: I just waited through the heat until dawn, my bed right next to the window, my head a foot from the screen. I could vaguely smell the tar-papered roof, cool breezes would blow in from time to time, the trees would heave up in a big hush. I could hear the nighthawks up in the sky above. Keats "Ode to a Nightingale" — how many generations of night-hawks have come and gone since I lay all night next to an open window just like this, when I was a kid in Chicago, listening to these same birds?

Either I'm goofy or Christine still loves me, wants back, wants it all back the way it was — including Tanya. Wants to be here! Of course, I forget that this may be the last good-bye, no more possibilities. And she must have felt that too.

She held on so long and hard.

I told Twyla: "Stay up here too, if you want."

"It's O.K. with me," said Christine.

Twyla smiled, laughed, got embarrassed: "I'd like to, really, it's always been so much more *intense*."

But she's not staying, and the dream of my seeing Amy coming up and going to school here is ended too, the dream of seeing it all happen. Job Agonistes.

Amazing how well Chris is swimming, jumping off the diving board. Tebida and his sisters come every morning to swimming class too now. I like the contrast between black and white skins in the early morning light.

Francis and I talk. She was telling me about her childhood in Kampala today. Her father was Minister of Agriculture. She remembers a big, cavernous house and lots of servants. I think of her mainly as "foreign," her blackness just a bass chord background that's "there," but you have to listen for it. She could just as well be Tunisian or Nigerian, Pakistani or Persian — or Hungarian, for all the difference it makes to me. Even the kids are so obviously non-American, a certain stiff angularity to their walk, nothing loose or hip or cool about them. Kind of formal little dorks. Totally different style.

Then I went over to the office to pick up my mail. A bunch of rejections. The usual: THE IOWA REVIEW, ANTIOCH, all the "in" places. And THE NIHILIST REVIEW took a couple of poems about Christine — *wir haben nur einmal, einmal gewesen zu sein*. Once, once, if you could only hold that Reality in front of you full-time — *einmal, einmal zu sein*, once, once to be.

Val looked good. Married to this white FBI-something-or-other now. More and more together. Clothes, face, expression. Centered.

"So how's it going?" she asked.

"Well, you know, I've been benched."

"Do I know? I could tell you stories about that, believe me! And how are you taking it?"

"O.K., a few last things to get in order. I'm gonna miss you."

Stops. All the professionalism crumbles for a moment and she's just a big, beautiful black woman with big, sad eyes.

"Likewise."

As if you can "miss" on the other side of the Veil...

And then I'm out. Let the boy see how I do my good-byes, who/what counts and doesn't.

On the way out remembering how it had been with Barry Sileski, the Assistant Chairman of the Department, the year before, before prostate cancer, then the bladder, then into his bones, until the bones got so cancer-weakened that they began to break if he walked, and he ended up in a wheelchair, still coming to his office every day, living on radiation, chemotherapy and liquid morphine. Until finally one day he simply didn't come.

He saw himself as heroic, and lots of people agreed. But I always saw the final siege as grotesque and ghoulish — the Phantom of Winthrop Hall.

Then a slow funeral march home with the kid, my arm around his shoulder, past the computer building where we used to spend lots and lots of time just nosing around, mega-computers and mini-computers, graphics and sound, even an artificial voice lab for people who couldn't talk without electronic help.

Then past Olds Hall. The fourth floor skull-collection used to spook him out. ("A little lesson in physical anthropology!" "Let's get out of here!") Past the library. He couldn't believe how many books I'd found on horror films, monsters, all his favorite stuff.

We'd take the books into my carrel overlooking the front trees and the bell tower (Beamont Tower), green in summer, white in winter, the perfect spot for the Observer of Seasons. We'd pour over them, make xeroxes and overhead transparencies, take them over to Bessey Hall, to the mega-classroom, project them onto a screen. King Kong, Godzilla, Freddy, Jason...

I'd take Varese or Berio or Berg, never without a camcorder and a cassette-player... these endless videos of us playing image-games over the years...

I had a video at home waiting for him — Andre Previn and the London Philharmonic doing Shostakovich's 5th.

"If you sit and watch this with me, I'll buy you another Batman T-shirt. What do you think?"

"O.K." And he didn't stir during the whole tape.

Debussy as a boy, his father putting coins on the piano keys in order to get him to play. How you get them there doesn't count, all that counts is the getting.

The third movement fooled me. Third movements are supposed to be pizzicato (Tchaikovsky's 4th), or at least scherzos. But this one, like most of the rest of the symphony, is pure lower depths melancholia — meditation.

Phone rings.

"I'll get it," says Chris.

A reprieve.

Only I get it.

"Hi, I just got back last night."

Howard Fine. He was supposed to be in Oregon for a sabbatical year. Since last September. At his sister's in Boring, Oregon. Always got a kick out of the name.

A letter every couple of weeks, a phone call now and then.

A serious maniac. Maybe a little too Henry Jamesish, pompous, especially since he discovered his grandmother had been Jewish. But totally talkable-to. No masks.

"Come on over," I tell him.

"O.K. How you doing?"

He was supposed to be back in the Fall, about two months from now.

"So when did Tanya call you?" I ask.

"I'll be right over."

And when he comes in the door, he's not very good at concealing the shock at how I look. Golden Boy, Beowulf, the Fat Man (Nero Wolfe) turned into Bone Soup...

"How long do you have?"

No frills.

"I thought you already got the whole story," I say sarcastically.

"What about...?" He nods Chris's way.

His Shostakovich over now, he's playing Rastan. Nonstop, seamless action.

"I guess when I finally go down he goes home, it's kind of open-ended."

"Home," as if this wasn't his home, just some pit stop, wayside shrine. Funny I should think/write that — wayside shrine.

*****

Fine stayed until 4:30, and then I had to pick up Tanya at the hospital. I guess I'll see him every day. I wish I could see the others, all the others, Lynne Savitt and Larry Kopf and the two Charlies, Potts and Plymell, the two Bennetts, John M. and just John, Blythe Ayne, Diane Kruchkow, Pyros, D.R. Wagner, Ingrid Swanberg, Horse Morse... all the visionary, hop-head holy ones from the Last Jamboree in Berkeley in

April of 1968. The resurrection of the dead — D.A. Levy and William Wantling, Sidney Bernard, Menke Katz... the Armageddon of the poets at the end of the world.

When I picked up Tanya and told her that Fine had been over, she closed up a little. Busy. Busy behind my back. What's the point? Of course, I was glad she'd called him, but...

"When are you taking off work?" I asked her.

"Wednesday. Indefinite leave."

"So you won't rush me."

No answer.

"I'd like to go down to Chicago and see my cousins and Aunt Trudy."

An "O.K." with a negative twist on it.

"You don't think I can make it?"

"Do you?"

TUESDAY — JULY 4
HOLIDAY PICNIC

Out to Fine's place in Okemos for a July 4th picnic. Margarita up from Farmington Hills for a visit — without her husband. No questions asked, but she volunteered, "He went up North with the guys — moose-hunting... without guns."

So it begins.

When Fine first bought his place out in Okemos, it was almost wilderness-area/swamp. Then they built the Meridian Mall, then extra satellite shopping centers. So that now his place is hidden in a strand of trees sandwiched between Harry Holden Chevrolet and a discount appliance mart.

He always peoples his place with weirdo exotiques. One tall beige drink of water in Chinese history who's just on her

way to Beijing to "fine-tune" (as she put it) her Chinese, then
an enormous sausage-armed fatso with red hair and pink
eyes, covered with freckles, like a freckled albino guinea pig (a
sports reporter for some newspaper in Grand Rapids), then
another woman, all shiny and polished and "new," like a new
TV, a new car. With Silitron in Detroit. "It's a computer
installation, education and repair company." Margarita
instantly buddies with her: "I'm a computer supervisor for
the State of Michigan myself." And off they went with a
couple of guys with moustaches and red ties. Table on the
back of the property in the middle of a bunch of pines. And
I had a chance to talk to Fine a little.

"I'm thinking of going down to Chicago for a week or
so..."

"O.K."

Face drops.

"So you don't think I can make it either. How much
time does she give me?"

Tanya inside in the bathroom with Chris.

He hesitates, but...

"Not long."

"Not long enough to get to Chicago and back?"

"Why not!" he says, as Tanya comes out, catches our
mood, almost goes back in.

"Where's Margarita?"

"Out with the Yuppies. Her usual," I smile.

Like this apartment complex she lives in in Farmington
Hills, a part of this whole Yuppie satellite world circled
around Detroit, self-contained moon-colonies.

"Brian was just telling me about his plans to go down to
Chicago."

"How about Chile?" I say, kidding and not kidding.

Really, if I had one place I'd like to go to die, it'd be the
Atacama Desert in Chile. San Pedro de Atacama. Go out

into the desert, up to the Loma Negra, this stone-age imple-
ment-cluttered butte where the Puripica and Puritama rivers
meet, right on the Tropic of Cancer. If I could make it to the
third week of December, go to the Solstice Point at the
summer solstice, watch the sun stand still and then turn and
begin a new year...

Sun worship is the only religion that makes any sense to
me, not Christs or Buddhas or Adonais, just sun and stars and
planets, wishful-thinking celestial-clock metaphors of death and
resurrection.

Funny afternoon. The Yuppies came back into the fold,
Margarita happy as hell, and then around dusk all the writers
in town began to show: Diane Wakoski, Diane and Marcus
Kafagna, Paul Somers, Leonore and Roger Smith, Sheri and
Dick Thomas, Etta and Herb Greenberg, Maria Holly, Smolens
and his beautifully spooky tall wraith of a wife... I always
forget her name.

All well-orchestrated. You could depend on Fine to do
that.

Never too close to any of them. They aren't people you
can get close to. All introverted and self-involved, although...
although... although... two layers down and they're the most
sensitive people in town. They came to Le Tombeau de
Couperin, didn't they?

Crazy, the idea of "making it" as a writer or anything else
seems so remote right now. And even if you "make it,"
exactly what do you make? Rimbaud, Hopkins, Baudelaire.
Make it into Special Collections, the Rare Book Room.

Then the fireworks went off and the wind turned and we
were all swallowed up in smoke. Another perfect metaphor.

Then everyone saying goodbye, keeping it aloft, aloof,
distanced — but you could feel it anyhow.

I've always loved Etta in a way. Right out of Klimt. And
Herb a kind of Freud-Bloom (Joyce critic). And Dick Thomas

always "there" over the years, reacting, receptive, and Leonore with all her own genetic quirks (mental problems in her family too) always warm, the same with Roger. What the hell, two decades, I could have done worse, one moment of unity with my Hippy Saints in Berkeley in 1968, and the rest of my life with poet-scholars.

The goodbyes full of overtones of finalities.

I had rented *Tosca* for tonight for the boy, but when we got home, it was much too late. And it was up to my space-ship room, lying on the bed naked, thinking how I was last summer, after my gallbladder operation, seven stories up, glass-walled hospital, looking down, sitting in the hallway between the two wings, listening (like now) to Delius's Cello Concerto (Jacqueline De Pres, already long dead too), the building disappearing, floating out into the Mind of God... Mind... Mindlessness...

WEDNESDAY — JULY 5

Called my Cousin Georgie this morning.
    He couldn't believe the cancer-story, thought I was kidding.

Most on-target guy I've ever known. Nuthead mother but Buddha father... who'd probably still be alive if a blood clot in his leg (visible for years, he could have done something about it) hadn't let loose one day when he was out watering the lawn and bent over to disentangle the hose.

"Listen, we can come up there if..."

"No, that's O.K."

"How soon?"

"Tomorrow?"

"O.K. Call me at the office when you get a time. I'll pick you up. You've got the number, right?"

"Sure."

"O.K., pal, I'll call the Averys, let them know you're coming."

"O.K. See ya."

The Averys, my father's sister Rose's family. Four boys and one girl. Rose was Crazy Daisy's twin. And how crazy it was. Daisy had lived most of her life in a nut house, no kids. Rose had had five kids and lived "free." And they both died the same year, two years earlier — talk about genetic fatalism.

The Burnses and the Averys didn't get along too well. Families drift. Brothers and sisters are one thing, first cousins something else.

The only ones who had really stayed glued together were Georgy and his brother, Bobby. (Bobby's my age, Georgy two years younger.) But even they'd lost contact with their sister, Emily. Another crazy, in and out of the nuthouse too. Lives in Grand Rapids, about an hour from here. I haven't seen her for twenty-five years. Called her once and she wasn't home, her husband said, but Georgy told me that was the usual cover-story. She was there but didn't want to/couldn't talk to anyone.

Hadn't seen any of the Averys for, what, nineteen years. The last time was when I first met Christine and brought her down to Chicago to "meet the family," the only family I had, brotherless and sisterless the way I am and with things always bad between me and my parents. I wanted to hang on to something. I never understood why my parents couldn't just bask in the now, never just let it be, whatever it was, just let it BE. What the fuck was I supposed to be anyhow, their little trained poodle?

Fine over this afternoon.

"I don't want to overstay my welcome," he had to rub it in, "but as long as you're deserting me..."

Watched *Tosca* with Chris. He wants a *Terminator* T-shirt now.

"You're making goofy connections in his head," said Tanya, "when he grows up, every time he goes to a musical event he'll have to go out and get a T-shirt."

Ironically, he liked *Tosca*. More than I did. Scarpia's too transparent a character for me: "I am evil and enjoy doing evil things!" Even Chris said it: "He's kind of like Darth Vadar in *Star Wars*." And I'm afraid he is.

Last act. A boy soprano, something about the stars and his girlfriend. A little mood-piece which took off for me. I compared it to the Paris Gate scene in *La Bohème*. Which Chris remembered.

And then later on tonight, when we were watching the end of *The Dark Crystal*, where the evil Bird-People are united with their better selves, and I started talking about the better-self characters as just that, the Good Side of the split person-alities that were healed by the crystal, and said how their singing reminded me of Tibetan Buddhist monks, he got all interested. Starting to get fascinated by complexity.

After Fine had left (after coffee and bran muffins) I told the boy: "You're a wonderful boy, and you're going to be a wonderful man. Take my love with you the rest of your life."

And I took him upstairs. A whole wall full of records and CD's.

"This is yours, pal. You've gotta work into it, like breaking in a pair of new shoes."

Played a little of Saint Saens' Third Symphony, Messiaen's *Quartet for the End of Time*, bits and snatches of Prokofiev's Third and Fourth Piano Concertos, the third of Rachmani-noff's *Three Russian Songs*, Opus 41.

"You'd never believe what these songs are about by listening to them. Stupid stuff, really. A song about two ducks, a song about an abandoned bride and this one about a woman who's screwing around with someone else behind her husband's back. Great music on trivial texts. It can happen. Like Puccini."

Ironic that I have such a strong sense of SELF right now at the end. I know who I am, Cezanne inside the landscape, Rilke making himself totally passive to the secret voices of the *Dasein* all about him.[12]   Only what secrets? Deaths and Resurrections? Xipe-Totec/Jesus, the Spring-God? And what had Moses really seen on Sinai, God or ancient astronauts?[13]

Filled with a floating, half-extinguished Buddhistic sense of Godhead. Like the way I spent a lot of my childhood. Polio, then a year afterwards I fell down and cut up my left leg on broken milk bottles, then an appendix, a gallbladder, a broken arm. Now the final siege, each major sickness always filling me with a sense of resigned bewilderment.

Taking the dogs out into the backyard today, noticing the teleological, "thought-out" procession of change. The Tulips are just topped with little knobs, the strange alpine flowering "grass" that covered the ground in Spring now receded into memory, dandelions, after spewing out their seed-fluff, now withdrawn back into ugly insignificance, the trees sprouting into their glory, everything ordered and planned, Aziza in heat, a drop of urine and the whole neighborhood of dogs is alerted. I used to always kid Morse. Him and all his books on evolution:

"That evolution's really smart, brilliant."

---

12. *Dasein* — "Being there" in German.

13. Xipe Totec is the Aztec god of Spring/Renewal.

THURSDAY — JULY 13

B ack in East Lansing after my visit to Chicago. No attempt to write anything down while in Chicago. I finished every day practically crawling into bed.

One day (Friday? The whole thing vague and floating) the whole clan gathered at Georgy's place. Georgy, as usual, in his white (doctor's... although he's not a doctor) pants and shoes, with this piped-in gas barbecue, the ultimate in suburban cool at one time ten years ago, now just as ordinary as front doors... passé

Georgy all red-faced and overweight. The champion guzzler. Brother, does he stash away the whiskey and steak. He's a coronary waiting to happen.

Peggy (wife) still her perky, broken-mirror, shamrock self.

Bobby and Barbara (B and B) still a handsome couple. George has all his hair, Bobby's bald — and very aware of it. It's funny, their father (at 86) had a full red head of hair.

All the kids there, kids and kids' kids.

All the Averys there except Bessie. And crazy Emily wasn't there either, of course.

Jack Avery told me: "Bessie's down in Tennessee, that's where Nashville is, isn't it?" Big joke. "Second marriage, or is it her third? I get confused."

But I thought it was significant. Six boys there and the two girls not there — both loopy.

Jack Avery — a lawyer. His son a lawyer too, looking and sounding like lawyers.

Bill Avery — construction business. Four kids.

David Avery — another lawyer. Three kids with first wife, a little boy about Chris's age with his second wife.

Dick Avery — a high school coach, like his dead father. Two kids. Not there. In Colorado. Summer jobs.

All I'm left with is a kind of affable blur. I drank too much whiskey without even thinking about it. Had to find an upstairs bedroom and nap a while, woke up in the middle of this horrible dream — a little too close to waking reality — that I was a lung on a beach drying out on the sand under an ovenish sun.

Tanya kind of hovering around me the whole time. Came in and woke me up.

"Are you all right?"

"Maybe this wasn't the world's greatest idea."

"You want to just stay up here? I can take care of it for you."

"No, they all came. After all..."

So many embraces. So many kids — in their twenties! Faces telling me, "I've heard so much about you!"

All the family I'd always missed. How can you have 25 years of Christmases and Thanksgivings together and then nothing? Moving away. All my extra needs. All this bullshit about being the great artist. Images overlap. *In the beginning... The spirit upon the waters.* The books in Special Collections — as if they were my family.

I kept thinking the whole time that I shouldn't ever have left Chicago, not just because of cousins, but closed drawers of old friends. And then the thought of how different it would have been if my mother hadn't had an abortion before I was born, if she hadn't had her tubes tied off after she had a tubal pregnancy *after* I was born, if I'd had a brother or a sister, all my life surrounded by such a heavy sense of loneliness and isolation. Like the "distance" between my friends and me in East Lansing. No one seems to know what the fuck I'm talking about.

Like Dick Thomas has a sister down in Bloomington. A masseuse, kind of inert, non-functioning blubber — but she's there, off humming in the distance.

Trying to hang onto my kids — who don't (and they're right) want to be hung onto. Only I didn't feel lonely at Georgy's, not for a moment. As if my first twenty Thanksgivings and Christmases and Easters with them had resurrected. Of course, without my mother there this time. All my father's sisters (except Rose) were college graduates, and they never let my mother forget she wasn't. Which didn't help things, her always being treated like an inferior/outsider. Not that her having a degree would have changed anything. Or if they had treated her better. She has this built-in cast-a-pall-upon-everything mechanism functioning full-time.

Even the negative in families is existentially good, though. The Great Horror is cosmic loneliness/isolation. All that impersonal immensity that we (unsuccessfully) always try to personalize/anthropomorphize.

So tired right now. Increasingly hard to breathe. Tanya thinks that water is starting to accumulate in the pleural cavities, and they may have to go in and try to take it out with syringes.

But I want to get this down on paper, if for no one else but Chris. Everyone impressed by him. He's going to be O.K.

If I give him nothing else, I want him to have an urgency about Papa Bear, Mama Bear and the three (or more) Little Bears, flesh as rock, family as sanity. Primitive. Primal. Foxes and wolves. I want to wipe away the horrors he's lived through.

After a few days at Georgy's, we went up to Milwaukee to see Judy and Gene. I thought my mother may have wanted to meet me there. But, of course, she didn't. I don't think I'll make it to California. In fact, on the phone my mother didn't sound too encouraging as to my coming out there either.

"Now with Walter dead [the 10th 'victim' since my father died], my arthritis has flared up, congestive heart failure."

And if her perfect little baby boy's dying of lung cancer at 57, what does that make her in the eyes of her fellow 'inmates?'

Judy and Gene live in a Jeffersonian neo-classical Gone with the Wind dreamhouse mansion — big white ante-bellum columns and all. My Aunt Trudy, my Uncle Jake's wife, lives with them. Face cancer. The same as her mother. You look at one side and she's an 85-year-old surprisingly unwrinkled and hearty Kewpie Doll, and then she turns full-face and it's The Twilight Zone, one whole side of her face like yellow, melting wax.

About five years ago, when Jake died, she sent me a box of things out of my childhood — my first piano pieces, all held together with tape, not Scotch tape but prehistoric tape, tape from when I was a kid. Pictures of me — First Communion, graduation from grammar school, high school, college, wedding pictures. All the cards and letters I'd ever sent her over the years, all tied together with a faded, light lilac, lace-trimmed ribbon. She'd done more thinking about me over the years than I suppose I'd done about myself.

All of which came as a big surprise to me.

Although she and my Uncle Jake had meant so much to me. They'd lived down the block. My father was the Marsh-mallow, Jake was the Man, playing the nags, had his own jazz orchestra, Jake Coughlan and his Harmony Kings, slicked-down hair, little moustache, tux. He'd bowled, been a Little League coach, comedian. Used to work Chicago nightclubs as a walk-on comic after he broke his hand one night trying to punch Trudy and it didn't heal right and he couldn't play sax any more. And he worked full-time in the First National Bank in Chicago for forty years — almost as kind of a sideline.

And my father? It was like being an M.D. was *it!* You get the M.D. and stop playing the violin, stop reading, stop anything, just M.D. it through life, sit, eat, smoke.

My mother (the Czech) always hated Irish Trudy. But maybe not because she was Irish, but because she'd married her brother. The same as my Grandma — because Trudy had married her son.

Weird, radical, endogamous, xenophobic family, full of disdain, distrust, hatred of anyone outside the Clan.

Trudy liked Tanya.

Everyone liked her. Passive like a piece of brown plastic clay: you mould her the way you want, create the image you want.

Big bedroom upstairs for us. Wanted to put Chris in a separate room, but he wanted to stay with us.

Pool in back.

Gene a little skittish with me. Me and the two women, three wives. A little too experimental for his medieval tastes, I guess. And me being a professor, people always put off by professors/writers anyhow.

Anyhow, he's kind of a cold guy. Or maybe just normal, and *I'm* the bloody, bleeding wound.

Former alcoholic. Alcoholics Anonymous. Steelworker who went to night school and became a metallurgical engineer, ended up co-partners in a new steel mill rescued from the bankruptcy of the company he'd been working for.

Everything in the house duly expensive.

The holidays we didn't spend with my father's sisters, we spent with Judy and her parents.

And for a few moments it was almost as if the years hadn't passed.

Sitting out by the pool with Judy and Tanya, Gene off at the store with Tom, their oldest, the electrical engineer (unmarried; the other two, Debbie and Gene Jr., married; Debbie in Cleveland, Gene Jr. a dentist in Englewood, California.

Judy the same old simpatica, mindless, funny, fun person as ever. Big fat moonface. She doesn't laugh but booms like a circus drum. And booms a lot. Everything a big joke. The same as always.

"You know, you mom was here two years ago."

Of course, I knew. She wouldn't come to see me in Michigan, just across the lake, because I wasn't married to Tanya yet. At least that was the cover story. The fact was (is) that whatever you want, she doesn't do, and the more you want it, the more adamant she is about not doing it. The more she gets to you, the more she loves it — a real sadist creep.

"How was she?"

"Pretty horrible. When we didn't have anything, Gene was just a dumb Pollock, but when she was here she kept saying we were putting on the dog. She brought Wallace with her, and she started bitching him out because he was in the room just above her, and when he went to bed at night, he'd drop his shoes on the floor (not that he can bend down anyhow!), and I told him 'Just don't pay any attention to her.' Oh, my God, you don't contradict Napoleon!"

He had a black Lincoln and she had a red BMW, there was a Spanish-speaking maid/cook who I spoke Spanish with full-time, everything in the house was white and gold. I don't know, it was totally overdone, but I loved it. The only thing I worried about was Chris spilling cranberry juice on a white carpet.

I caught Tanya and Judy talking together by the pool when I came out after a visit to the john.

Under cover. Hush-hush. Big secret.

They stopped when they saw me.

"She doesn't know!" I rasped out as heartily as I could manage.

"What?" asked Judy.

"How long I'm going to last. No one does," laughing, shifting into a hacking cough. No blood, but lots of pain. Got a chance to spend some time alone with Aunt Trudy up in her room.

Filled with *memento mori*. I couldn't believe she'd held on to all of Jake's old bowling trophies. A *Jake Coughlan and His Harmony Kings* poster up on the wall, Jake with his greased-down helmet of hair and pencil-thin moustache, looking more like Don Giovanni than the Irishman he considered himself.

He told me one time when I visited them in Tucson a couple of years before he died (prostate cancer), "I guess for an old Irishman, I haven't done too badly."

His father Irish, his mother (my grandmother) Czech. And she raised me (dumplings, sauerkraut, second-day bread/ vegetables/meat, second-day worldview) so that I always looked upon myself as Czech. And his gypsy look didn't come from Ireland. Put a bandanna on his head and a violin in his hand instead of a saxophone, and you'd have your quintessential gypsy violinist.

"We're in great shape, both of us, aren't we," Trudy said.

Forcing me to re-see her half-melting face that I was already beginning to forget about, see as normal.

"What the hell," I answered, "it's gotta come to an end sometime, I just wish I'd grabbed on to it a little harder. Lived it. Really LIVED it."

"Not just you," she said, "You know what I always wanted to be?"

I thought she was going to say "be a chorus girl, go to Vegas," that's the way I'd always seen her — as a Jazz Age doll, the only good-looking woman (except my mother, who

I also thought should have been in the movies) in the whole family. My father's side, forget it, they all looked like horses.

"I would have liked to have been a doctor, like your father. And now I see it could have been possible. Only back then it was all so limited, you couldn't see anything. No models..."

There were models, of course. The Number One student in my father's med school class was a woman — Dr. Gertrude Engbring. The same era as Ruth Benedict and Margaret Mead.

But those models were invisible in the shanty Irish southwest Chicago world from which Trudy had emerged like the Morning Star.

"I don't know, me and my typewriter, now word-processor, that's been my big love-affair. And I didn't 'make it.' And if I had? Farrell made it, Durrell made it, Virginia Woolf and Sappho and George Herbert. So? Hair today, bald tomorrow."

She didn't laugh.

"But it's different for you," she said, closing her eyes as if expecting a visit from the Holy Ghost: "At least you did what you wanted to do. You saw it and you did it. Most people, even if they see it, never even approach it."

The her that had never been.

Feeling dizzy, the bottom starting to drop out, feeling we ought to get a second time around at LIFE, once isn't fair, you just get your shoes on (or off) and...

"I think I'm gonna lie down for a few minutes."

"Need any help?"

"No, I can make it."

Not sure that I could.

"O.K., cutie, see you later," she said, laughing. Cutie? Like I was still five instead of five thousand. Maybe that's what I'd always be for her.

Walked up to my room feeling like I was already dead, come back to haunt the gold-white house. And I slept, that was the good part, the total rapture of the deepest sleep, when dreams are so real that when you wake up, the Other Reality seems like dream... hands around me, fluttering like blowing leaves, hero dream, and then Christine, always Christine, dream-versions of our real places, the Hotel Londres in Buenos Aires, and then later the Pension Londres in Santiago, our place in Valencia, Spain, in the artists' quarter, like living *La Bohème*, surrounded by the gang from Bellas Artes, our first place on Grove Street in East Lansing, our first tiny house in Okemos, always beds and hands and her black and green and red-stripped legs, me always on top of her before she vanishes. How many times have I awakened in the middle of the dark, crying. And when she was there I could reach over and she'd always hold on, like I was one of her long, lost kids...

I wonder what they all thought of me, all my cousins and their kids and wives.

And I was the one who came to every major holiday all spruced up like Beau Brummel, all during our shared growing-up, with a pretentious little something for the piano, or a new song or a new poem. And everyone else was baseball and football and swimming, Uncle Jack (Avery) was the big high-school coach and all the boys (and Bessie!) were big Neanderthal jocks, and there I was, the Young Mozart. Brother, did they love me!

Me and Morse. You can see why we're pals. Him and his chess computer. Nerds of a feather and all that...

4 A.M., UNABLE TO SLEEP

I've been calling Christine every night. And there are times when she's totally passive, "moist" with me.

"You're the most important person in the world for me, are, and always will be."

Her (I'm *certain*) feeling the same about me, but never, never, never saying it.

"I appreciate that a lot," never more than that, and always ending every conversation with "Say hello to Tanya," feeling *that* was revived too, ever since Christine's visit to Michigan.

Everything beautifully serene and open, and then two things happened: Amy got accepted at UMKC (U. of Missouri, Kansas City) and Mimi came back from Texas.

Simultaneous events.

So all of a sudden Amy definitely wasn't coming up here for school, which bothered me because I could get half-off on tuition for her because I'm on the faculty, and (mainly) because I've been looking forward SO MUCH to having her around for however long I've got.

I wanted to pay everything for her, and when Christine asked me for $700 to pay her fees until her loan came through, I got pissed and told Amy: "What's the point of your finishing college with a pile of debts down there when I can pay everything up here?"

And Amy started crying. Christine got back on the phone.

"Maybe it's better for you not to be calling down here. I can call you when I want to talk to Chris."

O.K. Only then she didn't call at all.

All my old paranoias surfacing. Of course, I was nasty, but... I don't know how Christine can stand Mimi at all with her bulging Japanese temple-demon eyes, always fidgety, at war with everyone in any lab she's ever worked in. Bitching out the postman, at war with the neighbors.

And Christine's still being in love with Tanya, how do you balance those two polar-opposite personalities? Christine'll never get over Tanya.

Christine should have never left East Lansing. It's her kind of place. Loved it in the Fall. And Spring. The library. She had her own carrel. A little glass crow's nest up above the trees.

Fucking Tanya, she could have continued to have a little sex with her, didn't have to get so "pure" all of a sudden. Get inside the marriage, fuck the wife, then get rid of her. All that stinking little mute manipulativeness.

Throw Christine to the dogs (Mimi). And then, all of a sudden, the Little Shop of (immunological) Horrors surfaces inside her. Tear glands drying up, then salivary glands. Like her father's connective tissue disintegrating. Another totally unfulfilled, unhappy stiff. Like father, like daughter. This slow sinking down into depression, death hanging over everything like a fog in an old Frankenstein film. And don't tell me there's no connection between her auto-immune problems and her personal life!

I told Christine a couple of weeks ago about Judy Beck killing herself. Old friend from grad school. Dead for three years, and the first I heard was a couple weeks ago back at the pool, talking to Dick Stauffer. All that permanent-temporary bullshit over at the university. No insurance, no retirement, no social security.

The same situation that Christine had been in for years.

And she was so hungry for details.

Tanya always says that Christine's too egocentric for suicide, but that's not the way I see her at all.

Here I am in the dawn's early light, sleeping for long eternities between words, longing for it all to come back together, like Poe's *Eureka*, the universe as contracting-expanding heartbeat. I know it's all getting disconnected on the page, but I can't seem to connect it any more...

FRIDAY — JULY 14

Slept all morning. Tanya took Chris to his swimming lesson and then picked me up, and we went to breakfast at MacDonald's next to Aladdin's Castle video-game arcade at Meridian Mall. Then we went over to the Potter Park Zoo. Wonderful new monkey-tiger-lemur building. Loved the spotted-tail lemurs.

"But what are they, monkeys?" asked Tanya.

"Dreams out of *The Dark Crystal*," I smiled, "but seriously, when they were trying to 'invent' animals in *The Dark Crystal*, they couldn't invent anything stranger than what is..."

The lemurs with their little fox (fruit-bat/fox-bat) faces and monkey bodies, the peahens (not cocks) with their antique brown-beige feathers with their pea-chicks following them around, the king vultures with their Boris Karloff techni-color skull-heads, the mandrills with their blue faces and blue and yellow asshair, as fine as feathers...

Glory be to God for dappled things,
for skies of couple-color, as a brindled cow,
for rose-moles all in stipple upon trout that swim...

Spacey, spaced... I dragged myself around through camel rides and pony rides, to the petting zoo (miniature African goats). Finally Chris started playing in the park, this multislide monster he used to play on when he was three and four, and

I kept remembering our year in Spain before he was born, 1975-1976, the zoo in Valencia, how I felt like the Buddha full-time. Christine had the job that year; I was just the prince consort. That's how you get to be the Buddha. Christine and me and the two girls.

"She'd give anything to be up here," Tanya said today about Christine.

Not really able to see what my dying's doing to everyone around me, a strength of ties that I can hardly even dream exists. Like Henry James — how could he have ever imagined, almost a hundred years after his death, me, Brian Buckley, re-reading/re-living his journals, that part about visiting the graveyard in Cambridge and thinking about his dead, facing the Horror and then pulling himself forcibly back, "*Basta, basta!* — Enough, enough!" How could he ever have imagined that there would have been a man who would have been moved by and sympathized with him a hundred years after he'd written what he'd written?!

I wonder what Christine is really feeling now.

Basta! Basta!

Like when I called Morse earlier this evening, Brenda answered:

"Brian, I was just thinking of you!"

Just a kind invention or for real?

Wanting so much to be thought of/loved. Tanya asking me today, "What do you *care* what Christine thinks or says?"

My answer, coming from way inside the center of it all:

"I don't know, my mother never once said 'I love you,' and the game was always 'If only you'd so something else/be someone else, *then* I'll love you,' only the *then* never came. I even remember a letter she sent me one time when I was in Argentina: 'I think you must be a changeling. Someone must have taken my real baby from the crib in the hospital and substituted you instead.' Dead serious. No joke. What are you supposed to do with that? I guess Christine's some kind of deep-down security for me, maybe that's what guys like us are always looking for — the mother we never had."

And, I could have added (but didn't): "The mother I can never find in you."

Thinking today about the last letter from Christine to me before Tanya came into the marriage: "I'm hungry for you. What we have defines marriage."

Her in Kansas City. Me in Brazil getting things set up, before her and the kids came down. And then she came — and met Tanya.

Fine stayed around until almost one.

"What about all your books, manuscripts?"

That was the theme of the evening.

"I suppose I could give everything to the library right now. Unless you want some things."

"No, I don't want anything. I was just thinking, all the krazy-kat novels and the poetry, you really ought to do something with the library. I can just see in the year 2032, the Centenary Edition of *The Works of Brian Buckley*."

Me thinking Amy will be 60, Christine 88... how a few years change everything.

Christine 18 — shy, isolated, introverted, brilliant.
Christine 25 — the wild woman, all juice, daring, fire.
Christine 35 — the matron, housewife, devourer of best-sellers.
Christine 40 — Lesbian/bisexual lover. Hot stuff. One-way, two-way, three-way, any way at all. And then Tanya said no, and we moved into...
Christine 45 — the Warrior Lesbian, pissed, isolated, defensive, still brilliant.

The joke of literary (or any other kind of) immortality. One time in New York, some kind of literary jamboree, I forget what, we were all in this bar in the village — Lynne Savitt, Lifshin, Paul Foreman, Morse, Larry Kopf, Sidney Bernard — and the waiter didn't know who we were but picked up on something (we had to be something weird), and he asked us: "Aren't you that country rock group that's playing down at the Purple Onion?" To which I answered: "No, we're The Spirit of 1968," which, in a sense, we were/are. Lost Hippy Shamans, the Riders of the Purple (Psychedelic) Sage, Amerikanski Priests of Amen Ra.

For me we've always been the Sons of Ben or the Surrealists or the French Impressionists, the Concord Mystics. I've always felt like Monet next to Renoir and Pissaro, or Clive Bell having lunch with Virginia Woolf, or Emerson sitting on a porch at sunset chewing the fat with Thoreau, or Bretón walking through the winter Paris streets with Aragon. At least I've had that. Trudy was right about that much.

New problems in my lungs.

The breathing becoming pure agony now. Little by little Tanya taking over all the functions of house and parenting.

Want to get Orson Welles's *Macbeth* tomorrow, and the Japanese version, *Throne of Blood*, but caring about different versions of *Macbeth* seems less and less important as other lights and other voices take over.

No more radiation now. The cancer's everywhere. Tanya wants me to go back to Bergman tomorrow. She's been such a klutz when it comes to me. She's always been that way, leaves the doctor in the lab. You'd think she'd have a stethoscope in the house. Although I guess I can visualize my laboring lungs working in an increasingly small space, lung-capacity way down, an increasing sense of drowning spaciness.

The words on this page are like clouds for me now...

I   BARELY   AM

BODY

ANYMORE

PURE   MIND   (SPIRIT)

SATURDAY — JULY 15
BRUCKNER, THROUGH A GLASS DARKLY

Stayed in bed most of the day today listening to a tape of Bruckner's 9th over and over again. Using a tape on my Walkman so I didn't have to get up and restart the CD.

Then over to Bergman's this afternoon. Fluid in the lungs, the pleural cavities filling up, like a sinking ship. What did Tanya call it, "pleural effusion."

They want to put me in the hospital full-time and try to get the fluid out with long needles.

Come on! Liquid Morphine, liquid sleep.

I still remember (age 4) the spinal injections when I had polio. Injections into the center of the soul.

Major medical and all. They're getting their bite of the whole thing.

"Can't we just, I don't know, go over to Muskegon, find a place on the beach, go down to Atacama or Buenos Aires or São Paulo," I kept lazily pleading.

Filled with these longings, the holy, shadowless, luminous, numinous Atacama Desert, the greatest paleolithic stone implement workshop in the world, or Buenos Aires, like Lautrec's Paris, old wood-walled cafés with old peeling mirrors, waiters who loved waiting, in black coats, white shirts and little bow ties. Or São Paulo, I remember going to a one-woman dance recital based on the work of Clarice Lispector. Hilly. Old theater. Old houses. Like Inglewood in Chicago, the Chicago Near North Side, Brooklyn Heights. I always seem to want to time-travel back either to the Pleistocene or the middle/end of the last century, the *fin de siecle*, when the real revolution began, Buddha Impressionists burrowing into an afternoon view of the Tuilleries and interfacing with Pleistocene Mystery.

That's what Bruckner's 9th says too — *through a glass darkly... and then you take away the glass.*

Tanya's answer to "why can't we just go somewhere where I can die in peace?" was "it's too late, that's what we should have done three years ago."

She's about as visionary as a can of cold sauerkraut. At the same time she holds on, is here.

Welles's *Macbeth* tonight. Chris liked it. Even though the language was 300 years out of date. And then I played the ending of *Throne of Blood*, the Martyrdom of Saint Sebastian arrow-scene. Which Chris really liked — the Japanese warrior-king transfixed with a thousand bloody arrows.

When he was four or five, I used to let him pick whatever he wanted to see at the video store — whatever! And he always picked things like *The Night of the Living Dead* or *The Return of the Living Dead* (one of my favorites, not a dead line in the whole script), and he'd always asked me to replay the parts where someone gets splattered all over the landscape. Loves blood, dismemberment, squashing, impalement, disemboweling, would have loved a sacrificial afternoon in old Tenochitlán.

But he never watches horror movies any more because they actually began to take over his mind. Beyond dreaming, replaying through his head all day long. So his mother put a quarantine on them — *verboten.*

O.K., but the itch is still there. We are what we are what we are, and I think he'll eventually end up making horror films, the same way Amy will end up as a movie star and Twyla will end up as a stand-up comedian.

Couldn't sleep so at 4 a.m. I got up and came down to watch the video film I'd done of them on Twyla's birthday over at the club. She's turned into such a beauty. All three of them bigger than lifesize. The last three. The first three, with their spiritual pygmy mother...

SUNDAY — JULY 16TH

B ack to Sparrow again, the first of the serum-withdrawals today. Gave me some kind of pills, but Bergman made a big point of "we can't be constantly giving you pain-killers!"

Why not? That's about all there is left to kill!

I'm 40% here and 60% in the *mas allá.*[14]

Pensé que iba durar muito mais tempo, mas asi es...

Hay golpes en la vida tan duras, yo no sé...[15]

---

14. *Mas allá* — the Great Beyond.

15. First section in Portuguese: "I thought that I'd last much more time, but that's the way it is," then a quote from Cesar Vallejo's *Poemas humanas*: "There are blows in life so hard, I don't know." (Identification and translation by MSU Romance Language Professor L. Ungaro.)

MONDAY — JULY 17

I float between life and death now.
Howard was here most of the day. Christopher for a couple hours. I've got a TV by my bed. He watched Nickelodeon for a long time. Tanya off, taking care of him.
I *knew* that if I let the doctors get me in here I wouldn't last long. If I had gone off into the sunset, for crissake, I would have suffered less and lasted longer. I'm convinced! And someplace in the middle of Pará or Paraguay, I would have found the last of the Great Shamans, and he would have laid his hands on me and pumped me full of magic and...
Our Father Who Art in Nada, Nada be Thy Name!

TUESDAY — JULY 18

Injections of Tetracycline into the pleural cavity after they took the accumulating fluids out. The idea is to try to get the lung to adhere to the walls of the cavity. So that fluid won't be able to accumulate in the first place.
Such bullshit!
Guinea pig. "How else can they learn?" Tanya says. More bullshit!
I had an idea yesterday to write a kind of time-capsule Message to Whomever:

WHATEVER I DID, DO THE OPPOSITE, CLING TO THE GROUND. NEVER FEEL SECURE OR TAKE ANYTHING FOR GRANTED. WE ARE GHOSTS, OUR LIVES PURE ILLUSION.

4 A.M. — FIRST ENTRY WRITTEN BEFORE DAWN

Then Tanya came with Chris and stayed for a while watching TV. They're spending most of the time at the club and malls. The same routine as before, swimming and video games, time with Fay, the Iranian, and Tebida, the Ugandan.

Only I'm not in the picture — that's the only difference.

Then Christine came in about two. Tanya hadn't said anything about her coming, being in town, although she must have known.

Howard came by while Christine was here.

And they even seemed to get along.

I told Howard: "It's best that Chris leaves. What's the point of his witnessing this?"

Which he countered with: "What the point of his not witnessing it?"

6 p.m. Tried to eat some salisbury steak smothered in onions, but simply wasn't interested.

This page is becoming time-travel.

I write a sentence, start to formulate the next, glance at the clock, it's four, then I'm off for twenty minutes, an hour. I float back into myself, revive a little, breathing an agony, but I hardly notice it, I'm so doped up.

Twyla and Amy in the room with Christine today.

So glad they came.

Christine confused.

"Maybe I'll just stay with him here. I don't know what to do."

"Do you remember, in Spain," I asked her, "all those pictures I took of you in Moorish doorways. You looked more Spanish than the Spaniards themselves, that white tile skin and black, braided, tied-up-in-back mane of hair?"

Images sliding through my mind, Valencia, the circular city, how we'd walk for hours in the narrow, circular streets, bird cages up above hanging out of windows. Plants. All dream now. I closed my eyes with Christine sitting in front of me and we were in Spain again together with the two girls just beginning to learn to talk (first language, Spanish, I wanted that!). It was such a good year, 1975-76. The year Franco died.

Go back and chose the Good Year and walk into it, stretch it out, wrap it around ourselves and make it our lives. I could have gone back, started again, at any time. Why couldn't she? *Yo pudiera haber podido* (I could have done it). How my old buddy, Cecilia Guilarte, the Basque novelist, loved to play around with subjunctive and conditional tenses.

MIDNIGHT — Tanya came by about ten with Chris. The kid's an amazing realist. He accepts, accepts, accepts everything.

He should be here when I finally go. Take the message with him the rest of his life. Smoking (Aztec) mirrors, crystals, crystal skulls.

What was I saying earlier about a time-capsule message? Point One — Be!

Point two — There isn't any Point Two. Christine and I, when I think about the initial intensity and how it matured and then how we trivialized it, as if we had a thousand lives and loves to spare...

4 A.M. — Dreaming of Mexico just now, although I never was in Mexico with Christine, just Maria del Carmen. Taking Christine back with me into times before I met her, bringing her back to Chicago, bringing her back to Orchestra Hall and the Art Institute, those evenings when I'd get a box seat at Orchestra Hall and then go to Le Petite Gourmet in the Italian Courtyard after the concert. I knew the pianist, I'd come in and she'd play Debussy for me, "Reverie," something from *The Children's Corner Suite*, one of the Bilitus songs. A chill Spring evening, a fire in the fireplace, a little wine and late, late spaghetti supper, and then a walk along the Oak Street Beach.

Bringing her back to the Andes with me, to the beaches of Santa Catarina, down the Amazon, out from Manaus before the Apocalypse began, to Belém, catch a fair Lord Jim wind and sail over to Marajo, the Isle of the Dead, down to the Caribbean where the waves rise up like horses on their hind legs, where Amazon meets Ocean. Go out from the village of Machu Picchu at dawn, down to the thermal baths of the Inca, steam rising up in the early dawn light. Or walk out into the Atacama Desert summer solstice afternoon, and bathe in the liquid everywhereness of the shadowless light.

FRIDAY — JULY 21
LA VIDA ES SUEÑO

Midnight. Days pass now like hours. They've given up on the Tetracycline idea now. It was a horse's ass of an idea anyhow.

Chris left this morning. I could hardly talk but I held him in my arms the best I could.

Amy crying again, Christine crying, even Twyla.

"I don't want to take him away, but..."

"So don't," I said, "it's like all your life all you've ever done is what you say you don't want to do," and then the old stoic himself broke, and he started screaming that he didn't want to go, grabbing on to me, me all full of tubes, Tanya pulling him carefully off, and then they got him un-clasped and they all left and it all went blank for me. All the king's horses and all the king's men and all that...

Tanya here a lot, "waiting." Howard waiting. I feel this tremendous EMPTINESS. *La vida ES sueño.* Life IS a dream...

SUNDAY — JULY 23
CONFESSION

Fine got a priest for me today. They brought a Jesuit in from Detroit.

Why not?

I "confessed."

Why not? .

I confessed that I hadn't been to Confession, but I'd taken the boy to Communion since he'd made his first Communion three years earlier, and that I didn't believe in Confession anyhow any more, in fact didn't believe in Communion, but I took the boy to Communion Russian Uniate style anyhow because I thought the sense of 'ritual' would be good for him. Three wives and the crazy life I'd led — put that in your pipe and smoke it.

I began antagonistically and then warmed, not to the priest as priest, but to the man, one of those fat, transparent, guileless Irish faces. He could have been one of my old buddies at Loyola — Father Ryan or Father Pollard...

Te absolvo.

And that was it.

Whatever Force or Intelligence or Chance that invented the crocodile, the ring-tailed lemur, the giraffe (and my mother), could just as well have invented immortality.

I don't have any trouble with the big brass chord in Bruckner's 9th. It seems so simple...

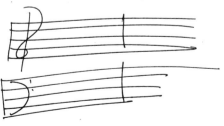

AFTERWORD

The diary ends here with the Bruckner chord not written in. The last entry was made the afternoon of the evening Brian died. When I typed up the final manuscript I was tempted to fill it in — I know what chord it was, he made he listen to it and look at it on the page enough times! — but in the end I decided to transcribe the diary just the way he'd left it.

So the diary ends up, not down.

Brian used to always say: "By the time we got to the Paleolithic we'd learned all there was to learn." Which to him meant a kind of polytheistic pantheism embedded in the Paleolithic metaphor of the solstice-year dying and then being reborn.

I feel I should say something about the influence of Menke Katz on Brian's whole way of seeing the world, especially in the last years of his life. It's odd that he hardly mentions Katz at all. I think the reason why is that Katz had become so much a part of him that it was no longer Katz but had become Buckley.

Before he'd gotten "bad," while he was still fluent, Brian had told me this about Katz's influence:

"Every time I've been to New York in the last twenty years, which is about three times a year, sixty times, O.K., Larry Kopf and I went and visited Menke Katz up in Glen Springs in the foothills of the Adirondacks. Larry is Menke's publisher. Menke's about 85. You've seen those vigorous old Jews; they're a special breed. He's a Kaballist, mystic, the only genuine holy man I've ever met. All he's ever done in his life is meditate, read, pray. Something like fifteen books published, Yiddish and English. Well, one day a few years ago, in the worst moments of the divorce, when

Chris simply wasn't functioning in school, I got talking to him about the problem, and here's what he said. You've gotta get the picture, long hair on the sides, bald on top, a thick Jewish-Lithuanian accent, these deep-set eyes, the man practically glowed with enthusiasm when he talked:

'My son, Dovid, didn't like to go to school either. So if he didn't want to go, I'd take off too. He liked busses. At first it was busses, later subways. So we'd go all over town on busses. That was when we still lived in Brooklyn. And every bus driver on Long Island knew us. «Hello, Dovid. Hello, Mr. Katz.» Dovid is David in Yiddish. To this day I've never spoken a word of English to the boy. I'd spend all day talking to him in Yiddish, telling him about Talmud, how King David was the greatest fucker of all time, how Solomon was a smuck, how Moses couldn't go to heaven because he denied he was a Jew. Kaballah. And then at night Rivka would come in and say: «Look, you're still going on, it's late, the boy will miss school tomorrow.» And I'd say: «It's not so late,» and I'd turn back the clock and tell him a little more about Talmud. And so it went. The boy's twenty-eight now. And what do you think he does?'

"Of course, I didn't know. The logical thing would be that he'd be a dropout, but...

'I give up,' I said. 'Well,' he answered, 'the boy's the head of the Yiddish Program at Oxford University.'

"And I started to cry. He wasn't taking the boy out of school at all, but turning his childhood into one long meditation in Yiddish. He was turning the boy into a great Rabbi like himself."

I'd only seen Brian cry like that one other time, one night out at my place in the middle of the Winter, just the two of us in front of a fireplace full of cedar logs, the whole house smelling like a vast cedar closet. He'd been talking about his grandmother, how his mother had always wanted him to be like some perfect, unreal, imaginary English heir-apparent, English clothes, even English soaps. And then she'd left him all the time with his old, barely literate Czech grandmother who was a real peasant. And that's what he'd become. He said he walked like his grandmother, talked like her, saw the world like a little village the way she did, even ate the way she did, the Czech kitchen, sauerkraut and onions and roast duck, roast pork.

"And then I left Chicago when I was 23," he said, "went to California, and didn't see her for, what, 15 years..."

That's when he broke down. He saw her when she was 92, just before she died.

"She was living with her son, my mother's brother, out in Arizona. I walked into her bedroom. She had terrible varicose veins, used to always wear rubber bandages around her legs. Only she didn't have them on. Bare legs. And they didn't look that bad. I came in, she looked up: 'Little Brian, I wouldn't know you, are you married? Any boys?' That was funny. 'Any boys?' The Old Country chauvinism. I talked to her for a while, then went into the bathroom and cried like I'd never cried before in my life. That went on the whole time I was there. I'd break down in the bathroom, then come out, we'd talk again. I remember, she took two quarters and tied them together with a rubber band and put them in her coin purse. 'Let's see if they have puppies.' I stayed for two days. She died about six months

later, all full of tubes, in a coma. My uncle told them to pull all the tubes out, let her have her dignity, something like that. She raised me — and then I got too busy with my own life and forgot about her. Only not really. I still walk like her, think like her. In a way she's still alive in me. And that's the way I want it to be with my boy. I'll be dead, but I'll still be alive in him. There's your real immortality!"

His Mount Hope.
I don't know if I'll ever see the boy when he's grown. My ties weren't with Brian's women but with Brian. But I did get a chance to see Twyla and Amy, his fifteen- and seventeen-year-old daughters, when Christine came up to take Chris back to Kansas. Twyla was full-time drawing and reading O'Neill, Amy was reading Rilke and running after anything with hair on its chest.

They were both big and beautiful, and I imagine the kind of aristocratic "selfness" they radiated was exactly what Brian's mother had wanted from Brian. Although I doubt that she would have seen it even if it was right there in front of her. That's the way the old crocodile was (and I've met her twice) — totally in her own head.

That's the way most of us are. It's not very often that someone steps out of his head and sees the Now for what it really is, or what it might become.

H.F.

Hugh Fox is a professor of American Thought and Language, a specialist in pre-Columbian Amerindian religion and a prolific writer. He teaches at Michigan State University, does research in Latin America and publishes fiction and non-fiction with houses big and small. His early titles include *Glyphs* (Fat Frog Press, 1969), *The Ecological Suicide Bus* (Camels Coming, 1970), *Paralytic Grandpa Dream Secretions* (Morgan, 1971), *The Gods of the Cataclysm* (Harper's, 1976) and *First Fire: Central and South American Indian Poetry* (Doubleday, 1978). His more recent titles include the novel *Leviathan: An Indian Ocean Whale Herd Journal* (Carpenter, 1980), the novel *Shaman* (Permeable, 1993) and *The Living Underground: The Prose Anthology* (Whitson, 1994). Of *The Gods of the Cataclysm*, a study of plumed serpents, yogic yantras and Mayan hieroglyphs, Curt Johnson wrote that it "ought to be required reading for cultural historians of all disciplines." Of *Leviathan*, the *Library Journal* found that "Fox's musings on man as the killer animal are often chilling." The *Small Press Review* called *Shaman* "quite simply a masterpiece... so original that it is hard to fit into any category." Fox is a contributing editor to numerous literary journals and, since 1968, the editor of *Ghost Dance: The International Quarterly of Experimental Poetry*.

Fox got the idea for *The Last Summer* when his ten-year-old son came to spend the summer with him in Michigan a few years ago and Fox broke his ankle in the first week. Rather than send the boy back to his mother in Kansas, Fox had a "walking cast" made and hobbled around with the boy for three months. Fox's lawyer friend, Jerry Beckwith, had died from lung cancer the year before, and Fox conceived the idea of turning the broken ankle into lung cancer and writing the story of a dying father spending his last summer with his youngest child. Before writing, Fox frequented the radiation department at the hospital where his wife, a pathologist, works. During the writing, he drew on his own medical background (four years before turning to literature) and his experience of sitting at the bedside of Jerry.

The diary technique is the same as used in *Leviathan*, a story of survival on the high ocean, also ending in disaster. "With this technique," says Fox, "the reader gets inside the head of the protagonist. It's the closest you can get to virtual reality on the printed page. I carried around a notebook the whole summer and wrote it as it happened. I have no mercy on the reader — or on myself."

Other XENOS BOOKS of interest:

Alfredo de Palchi, *The Scorpion's Dark Dance*, translated from the Italian by Sonia Raiziss. A bilingual edition of *La buia danza di scorpione*. "His poems are painful and exalting to read." James Dickey.

Imre Oravecz, *When You Became She*, translated from the Hungarian by Bruce Berlind. A cycle of prose poems detailing an obsessive love; it sold out within hours after its original publication in Hungary.

Vicente Huidobro, *The Poet Is a Little God*, translated from the Spanish by Jorge García-Gómez. A bilingual edition of major works by the experimental Chilean poet: *El Espejo de Agua/The Water Mirror*, *Poemas Articos/Arctic Poems* and *Ecuatorial/Equatorial*.

Forthcoming:

Antonio Di Benedetto, *Animal World*, translated from the Spanish by H. E. Francis. A bilingual edition of *Mundo animal*, a collection of short stories by an acknowledged Argentinian master.

Mario Azzopardi, *Naked As Water*, translated from the Maltese by Grazio Falzon. Collected poems of a bold avant-garde author.

Francis Carco, *Streetcorners*, translated from the French by Gilbert Alter-Gilbert. A bilingual edition of decadent vignettes by a demi-monde author.

Fabio Morábito, *Toolbox*, translated from the Spanish by Geoff Hargreaves. A bilingual edition of *Caja de herramientas*, a series of unusual reflections on the nature of things by a young Mexican writer.

Alfredo de Palchi, *Anonymous Constellation*, translated from the Italian by Sonia Raiziss. A bilingual edition of a collection by the New York Italian poet.